ALASKAN MAIL–ORDER BRIDE

an Alaskan romance
by Ted H. Leonard

illustrations and cover by Karen Farrell

ALASKA WORDWORKS PUBLISHING COMPANY
Salcha, Alaska

PUBLISHED BY ALASKA WORD WORKS
PUBLISHING COMPANY
PO BOX 51
SALCHA ALASKA 99714

This is a work of fiction. All characters and events portrayed in this book are fictional, and any resemblance to real people or incidents is purely co-incidental.

First printing September, 1996 USA

Library of Congress Catalog Card Number 95-081186
ISBN 0-9641553-2-X

Dedicated

with love, to my daughter, "Little Plum"... A.K.A. Amy Moeller.

Acknowledgements

Many thanks to freelance editor Ann Chandonnet for her help in preparation and her many constructive suggestions.

Thanks also to my family and friends for their continued support.

And thanks to Karen Farrell for a fine job on the cover and illustrations. Karen's illustrations appear on pages 7, 10, 37, 53, 76, 90 and 135.

CHAPTER ONE

Gold crowned birch clustered along the creek, highlighting crimson splashes of currant brush. Annie followed the winding, dirt path into the grove and stepped out onto the log bridge.

There, she paused savoring the sunlight that glistened from the rippling surface. In the crystalline depths, a motion caught her eye. A fish... several fish. Arctic grayling. A sense of quiet contentment enveloped her. What a lovely, peaceful place to live.

In the clearing ahead, she saw Kent bent over, sawing a downed tree trunk into stove-length pieces – winter firewood.

As he straightened, moving to the next downed birch, she caught his eye and waved happily. The sound of the idling saw stopped and, grinning broadly, he waved back to her.

Eagerly, Annie hastened forward, then halted, sensing the barest flicker of motion in the forest. She stared intently. Almost, she convinced herself that she had imagined it. But no, she saw it again. Something large and black moved – there, off to the right. Her pulse raced with the beginnings of alarm.

She peered through the underbrush. What was it? There! Yes, definitely an animal... a grizzly bear, just as Kent had warned. Why hadn't she brought the gun? There was the distinctive hump, the massive head. Her nostrils quivered at the stench, a heavy mixture of strong sweat, rotten salmon, and skunk-like musk.

A chill shuddered up her spine and her hair bristled, trying to stand erect. Her heart thundered in her ears.

Should she run? Her legs seemed frozen. Her breath rasped in her throat– shallow, dry gasps. Why hadn't she listened to him? Dimly, she became aware of someone screaming.

Who was that screaming? – Was it her?

For frozen moments she and the bear looked at each other... moments that seemed hours. Their eyes locked. She stared into simmering depths, seeing herself reflected there as meat... just meat.

Pure, evil rage crossed the bear's face, making him look like a devil. The skin on his nose wrinkled and his eyes narrowed, as he curled back his lips and bared his fangs in a snarl. The muscles of his fore-legs bunched and his shoulders rippled as he tensed to spring.

"Oh *God*! Don't let me die this way," Annie prayed fervently. Her dry tongue rasped her lips.

Suddenly, the bear flinched back, confused by Kent's running arrival on the scene to stand between her and the bear.

"Keep behind me!" Kent shouted. Two deafening gun shots blasted out. Kent was firing over the bear's head.

Now the grizzly stood erect, his head towering ten feet above the ground, and roared a challenge. His forepaws spread wide, reaching. He took a ponderous step forward, and another, massive and menacing.

Her heart was going to burst... it hammered against her ribs. Pungent, burnt gun powder filled her nostrils, drowning out the vile odor of the bear. Her ears rang.

By now the bear stood only twenty feet from Kent – but Kent stood his ground and fired another shot over the bear's head.

"Get!" he shouted. "Don't make me kill you! Go on, get."

The bear flinched from the muzzle blast.Then, unhurriedly, it dropped to all fours, turned, and shuffled off into the forest. Kent watched him go, then turned to Annie.

She set down the lunch hamper and bag of cookies that she had clutched tightly throughout the incident. Her legs felt weak and weakness washed over her whole body, the sickly aftermath of an adrenalin high.

Waveringly, she held out her arms to him. She badly needed some cuddling and comforting.

She must apologize to him and promise to heed his warnings in the future. He had been right and she should have listened. She felt humbled, humiliated by her own stupidity.

His courage in standing his ground before the bear, gave her a new

appreciation of his manliness.

Kent's fear and relief had turned to anger.

"Where the hell is your gun?" he shouted. "Didn't I tell you never to leave the clearing without it?" He stood panting and glaring at her, the rush of adrenalin subsiding in him, too.

Still highly charged with emotion, he said, in a scornful voice trembling with emotion, "Your disobedience and stupidity nearly got us both killed."

Stunned, Annie let her arms drop. She knew that he was right, but this was not the way a man who loves you should talk after you have been terrified and nearly eaten. Especially after only three days of marriage.

Tears of rage and sorrow rolled from her eyes. "I was just bringing you your stupid damned lunch," she screamed, feeling hysteria rising again. "You unfeeling brute."

He made a motion to touch her, perhaps to take her into his arms.

"Don't touch me!" she shrieked, slapping at his hands. Sobbing, she stumbled blindly back along the path toward the cabin.

As she burst from the brush, to run across the clearing and into her cabin, she could see him following her. He had better stay away from her, the brute.

She threw the door shut behind her with a soul satisfying bang. Damn him! Damn him!

Her bedroom door, too, crashed shut behind her, as she threw herself down on the bed. There she lay, gulping and sobbing until the waves of fear and anger began to recede.

Kent was an insensitive, unfeeling brute, she thought hysterically. Just when she most needed his love and support, he had turned on her.

Too bad she couldn't talk to Maggie... tell her about it. Maggie would know what to do. But Maggie was at Blaine's, five miles away, down a winding dirt path through the bush.

Annie was thoroughly trapped. And she had done it to herself. How could she have been so stupid as to get herself into this mess? Damn! Damn! She had just let herself fall into it – like some spineless little ninny.

Angrily, she damned herself, then settled into the soothing darkness of the room, pulling the quilt over her.

Worn out by the stressful events of the day, Annie faded into drowsiness... could it have been only a year ago that her secure life fell apart?... only a year ago... Elizabeth Anne dropped off to sleep and that year faded away. In her dreams she traveled back... back a year, to the events that had changed her life...

...The prairie wind sighed around her slight figure, ruffling honey toned, tawny hair, where it projected from under the brim of a black hat, and causing the black skirt to billow.

In a diffused glow of golden light, the Midwestern summer sun outlined her figure as she stood alone, gazing at the fresh dug graves. They were covered with flowers. At their head, a floral wreath bore a white ribbon imprinted *NELS AND DEBRA JENSEN – BELOVED FATHER AND MOTHER.*

Off to one side, stood a man, the only other person in the church yard, the rest of the mourners having dispersed to go on about their daily business. Life, after all, goes on.

The man stirred now, at the edge of her awareness, and came to stand beside her. "Elizabeth," he said.

Slowly, she turned, letting her tear-reddened eyes sweep over him. She saw a big, muscular man, slow-moving and slow-thinking but a kind and considerate neighbor. Just now, she saw, his brow was furrowed with a genuine and grave concern.

His voice was quiet. "You've lingered here a fair spell. The others left over an hour ago."

Silent moments lengthened. With unconscious habit, her teeth caught her lower lip, gnawing it gently.

"You're young, Elizabeth, only twenty-one." he spoke gruffly, "I know it's hard... coping with the loss of both your folks at once. But

you must keep on, not bury your soul in their graves. They wouldn't want that."

She nodded.

"I know." Her words came in a whisper. It seemed that she struggled to force them past an enormous lump in her throat. It was time to go. To linger would be unhealthy.

"Time to go," she said it slowly, musing, "Time to leave Mom and Dad here, hard as it is – time to go back to that lonely farm house, to think... to figure out what I should do."

A stronger gust of wind tugged at her hat, causing her to snatch the brim and pull it down more firmly. A dust devil whirled across the cemetery, ruffling the leaves of the lone cottonwood. It danced briefly on the graves, stirring a cloud of dust from the loose earth.

Placing her hand on his arm, she said, "All right Clyde, please take me home."

He nodded and led her away to his pickup truck, helping her in with a grave, natural courtesy.

During the silent ride home, she tried to come to grips with the sudden change. Her parents had both been still so young and vital, then their truck's tire had blown out and dumped them in the river to drown. It was all so sudden, so unfair. Most of all, so unexpected.

Fighting back tears, she struggled to banish the unwelcome image of their deaths in the river.

"They were holding hands, you know, when they found them." Her voice trailed off. They had been so in love... it seemed unfair, to chop them off that way. Senseless.

"It's best that they went together. Neither could have stood being left alone."

Clyde silently laid his right hand on her shoulder, evidently sensing her need for comfort.

"Look," he said, "The colts are playing." He nodded at the Iowa pasture flowing by outside their right window.

A smile tugged at the corner of her lips as she watched them frolic. The green of the meadow was dotted with wildflowers that gleamed, vivid yellow, in the sun.

Life did, after all, go on – like it or not – and so must hers, she supposed.

Clyde drove slowly, one handed. His face wore a gentle smile of affection, as he watched the young things play. He was born to be a farmer and loved all the creatures, especially the babies.

They reached her lane and Clyde turned down it. Bracing herself, she swayed with the motion, as the truck bounced along the rutted lane toward the grove of cottonwood trees that protected and hid the house.

They entered the grove and wound on through it, until the house came into view.

Snapping erect, she said, "What's that car there, near the front door?" It was long and black, a gleaming, ostentatious display of wealth. Who could it belong to? "I don't recognize it."

"Oh, oh! I don't recognize it either, but it doesn't look like the sort of car an honest person would drive," Clyde growled.

As they drew nearer, Elizabeth Anne could see a chauffeur behind the wheel and a passenger seated in the rear.

A foreboding of evil settled over her. Clyde was probably right. She strained to identify the passenger as they neared the car.

Clyde pulled up beside it and shut off the engine. Coming around, he helped her out of the truck. Together they faced the car, waiting.

A uniformed chauffeur opened the door, bowing slightly, she saw, as his master emerged – a tall individual, with carefully styled razor-cut hair, wearing an expensive-looking suit and a forbidding scowl.

What could he want with me? she wondered. Catching her lower lip between her teeth, she gnawed it worriedly.

"It is time someone was about," he snarled, "The day is half over. With a lackadaisical schedule like this, it's no wonder that this farm doesn't earn enough to pay its bills."

He glowered at Clyde. "Mr. Jensen?" He clutched a sheaf of papers in his right hand, tapping them impatiently against his left palm.

Clyde appeared taken aback. He pondered over the question, then slowly replied, "No... No I'm not Mr. Jensen. I'm Clyde Monroe." He shook his head. "We just buried Nels and Debra Jensen. They were killed in a car wreck."

Clyde looked at her, then at the man. "This is their daughter, Elizabeth Anne."

The man's expression changed from anger to uneasy distaste. He cleared his throat, glanced again at Clyde, then addressed himself to Elizabeth Anne.

"Young Lady," he said "I am Reginald Whitmire, the third, from Farmers National Bank. I regret the unfortunate timing but I have a notice of foreclosure and an eviction notice."

Silence stretched into a long moment. He studied her expression intently, evidently waiting some acknowledgement. Well, she was not about to give it to him. Her face felt strangely wooden, her mind numb.

When Reginald began to speak again, he looked a little shame-faced, she thought, if that was possible for this type of man.

He said, "Your father borrowed quite a large sum of money from my bank. Payments have become seriously in arrears. I presume that you were aware of that?"

Dry eyed and angry, she nodded. Reluctantly, she replied, "Yes. I knew. I expected to lose the farm. I just didn't expect the vultures to be already gathering on the day of the funeral."

A shadow of worry crossed her features, clouding her eyes. "How long do I have to get moved out?"

"I can give you one week." The anger was back in his voice and expression. "That comment about vultures was uncalled for. Banking must be handled in a business like fashion. But I assure you that I did not know about their deaths."

In a flat, emotionless sounding voice, Clyde said, "You have delivered your message, Mister. Now get out!" He looked calm and solid.

The banker studied Clyde and, wisely, decided against any further comment. Instead, he handed Elizabeth the papers, slid back into the car and slammed the door. He motioned to the chauffeur.

Moments later, the car lurched into motion and departed at high speed.

Brooding, she studied the dust of the departing car, already beginning to blow away upon the wind sighing through the cottonwoods. "This perpetual wind, blowing, blowing. Sometimes it's nearly enough to drive me crazy. That's one thing I won't miss!... But it was an ill wind that blew him in."

He scuffed his toe in the dust, looking embarrassed. Then he asked, "Your father had no life insurance?"

She shook her head. "No," she said. "Times were too hard after last summer's drought and Dad was young and healthy. He had to let the policy lapse, needed the money to buy seed and fertilizer for this year's crop of corn."

"What will you do now?"

"I just don't know. I've never made any decision without Daddy. Sometimes I've toyed with the thought of looking for work in the city. I don't think I would have ever have gotten up the nerve to go... but, I guess, the choice has been made for me now."

A resolute expression appeared on his face. Seeing it, she wondered what was in his mind.

"Elizabeth?" He appeared to be pondering something.

"Yes, Clyde." She waited patiently on his slow mental processes. How odd. He seemed to be blushing.

He studied her face, clearly plucking up his courage, and continued, "Elizabeth, I've always been very fond of you. Let me take care of you... I know I'm not handsome or very smart, and I'm older than you, but I would love you and take care of you. I'm a good farmer and you would never want for anything."

There was a beautiful expression in his eyes as he said, "I'm making bold to ask you to be my wife." He looked at her hopefully.

It had been a long speech from him, usually a man of few words.

Silently, she cast her eyes down. What a stunning development. She could not repay this gentle giant's kindness with hurt. But a marriage between them could not work... she needed someone who could stimulate her mentally. Besides, he did not stir the sort of feelings of sensual excitement that a husband should.

And yet... the temptation nearly overcame her better judgement. Security – and affection. It was *something*, better than many women ever get. Financial security, too; Dad had always taken care of that – 'though not very well, she thought, with a glance at the foreclosure papers... then damned herself for her disloyalty.

Tears welled in her eyes.

This was no time for a hasty decision. Elizabeth looked steadily into Clyde's clear, blue eyes and said frankly, "I don't know. I've never thought of you in that way. I... please... let me think about it until tomorrow."

Silently, he nodded. At his truck, he turned, to say, almost pleadingly, "I'll stop back tomorrow noon."

Elizabeth fled inside, away from the wind – and from thoughts of tomorrow.

Her parent's presence haunted the rooms. Dad's favorite chair, his pipe... Mom's flowered apron, hanging by the sink, as though she had just stepped out to pull some rhubarb and would be right back to begin a pie... A grocery list half done...

She fled to the sanctuary of her own room.

What would she do? she fretted. Vaguely, she had planned to go adventuring to the city, some day, and find a job. Maybe she should follow through with that. Then, there was Clyde's offer. Nothing else occurred to her.

It would be the easy way, marrying Clyde. After all, she fretted, she was only a high school graduate and her jobs skills could be listed on the fingers of one hand. Going off to Chicago was a big step, frightening.

She flung herself down on the bed, thoughts whirling until, at length, she dropped off into a gentle slumber. Her mind was busy while she slept.

As dawn's first golden light kissed her eyelids, Elizabeth stirred, wakened and rose, knowing what she must do. With a resolute purpose, she set to work sorting out mementoes to keep and packing them.

The clock gonged twelve times. Noon, all too soon. That sensitive area between her shoulder blades tingled, with a sense of being watched.

Startled, she whirled to find Clyde, standing outside the screen door, a soft look in his eyes. He did have tender feelings for her, she realized, with regret. But there must be no evasion, no ambiguity.

An honest man, he deserved honesty in return.

Crossing the room to him, she opened the screen to allow him in, then raised her eyes to look fully into his, placed her hands upon his shoulders, rose on her tiptoes and placed a gentle kiss upon his cheek.

"Clyde, I'm flattered by your offer – and tempted. But I can't accept, for I don't love you in the way a husband deserves."

He nodded, accepting her decision without argument.

"But what will you do?" he asked, obviously still concerned for her.

"I've decided to go to the Chicago and find a job," she said. "I'm packing my personal things and will go before the week is over. Jim, from the used shop, is coming today to buy the furniture and things. And the auctioneers are sending a man for the odds and ends of livestock. I'll get enough money to last until I find a job."

"And your pet calf, Sunbeam?" His expression was sympathetic.

Tears stung her eyes. Sunbeam was not just livestock, but a personality, a friend. "I can't take him with me. There would be no place to keep him, in the city."

Digging into his pocket, he sorted out some bills, handed them to her, and said, gruffly, "This is more than the auctioneer would give. I'll come get Sunbeam, after you leave, and give him a good home. At least, he won't go to the butcher shop. – You can visit any time."

He caught her hands in his. "If you ever need my help, let me know... anytime, now, or in the future."

Crossing the yard to his truck, he climbed in. He leaned out the window and said, "Good-by, Elizabeth." A sadness lingered in his eyes.

"Good-by, Clyde, and thank you."

She watched him drive out of the grove, then turned, with a sigh, back to her work – packing. There was a lot to do in a short time.

The week sped by, occupied by packing and bidding good-by to her friends and neighbors. Few, of her own age, remained for her to bid good-by.

Most of them had already left, rural economy being what it is these days. Family farms, almost a thing of the past, had been superceded by the mechanized, corporate factory farm... leaving few jobs to be had. Now her day to leave had come.

Elizabeth Anne stepped off the cross country bus and into the Chicago depot, an echoing, uninviting place. A chill ran up her spine. Fear churned uneasily in her stomach and her mouth went dry. She was stiff from the all day ride.

"Oh, help," she breathed. "Here I am in the big city. It doesn't seem such an adventure right now."

She breathed in deeply several times and severely told herself, "This *will* be an adventure and I *will* love it."

Taking a firm grip on the two suitcases that contained all her worldly possessions, she strode resolutely across the depot and out onto the busy sidewalks.

Rude strangers jostled her as she fought her way to the curb, seeking the sign for the city bus stop. Being short of funds, she had made reservations at an inexpensive hotel on the bus route.

The bustle and roar of traffic dazed her. All the buildings seemed depressingly dirty and drab. Heavy, dirty-looking clouds scudded across a sullen, grey sky. Swirling light winds carried bits of paper and debris along the gutters. The ever present wind. She hadn't escaped that by coming to the city.

"Taxi?" yelled the cabby parked at the curb.

She shook her head, thinking of her pitifully small hoard of money, and edged on down the curb to the sign that bore the route number of the bus she wanted.

Several buses came and went before one with her route number finally showed up. With dismay, she saw that all the seats were taken and the aisles were packed full with people standing.

The doors sighed open. “Squeeze it on back,” the bus driver ordered. “Come on! Come on, let these people in. Move on back.”

There was grumbling and shouted complaints but, by some miracle, space appeared for Elizabeth and the others who had been waiting at the stop.

At each stop down the line the scene was repeated. She found herself so jammed in that she feared she would suffocate. Her arms felt as though they would drop off and her legs grew numb.

At least, if she fainted, she wouldn’t have to worry about falling over, she thought wryly, there wasn’t room. The press of surrounding bodies would hold her up. She giggled hysterically.

Finally, people began to get off. A seat near her was vacated, and she slid into it with relief, earning a disgusted look from the hearty-looking young man who had been trying to beat her there. She felt pleased.

The victory of the seat was hollow, though, for the next stop turned out to be hers. The young man sneered at her as he dropped into the seat she had vacated.

Struggling off the bus with her luggage, she stared in dismay at the street she found herself on. Dirty and crowded, it was lavishly endowed with signs flashing *“GIRLS - GIRLS - GIRLS.” “NAKED LUST - SEE IT NOW.” “ADULT THEATER - XXX RATED”.*

The hotel looked no better than the rest of the dingy buildings. In front of it, a crowd of hoodlums leaned against the walls, whistling and catcalling at passing girls. Their long, dirty hair straggled about their faces and collars.

She was dismayed but she had no place else to go tonight. Eyes front, fixed firmly on the lobby door, she grasped her suitcases and strode toward the hotel.

Their eyes tore the clothes from her, leaving her feeling violated. They called out indecent proposals and propositions.

She would not give the punks the satisfaction of paying them any attention, she vowed, but her cheeks burned hot as she let the heavy door sigh closed behind her and fled across the threadbare carpet toward the battered front desk. There was an oppressive odor of... mildew?... or something. Her nose twitched.

The desk clerk was bored and slovenly. As she signed the register, he worked a toothpick in his teeth and insolently ran his eyes over her breasts and down, letting them follow the curve of her narrow waist and swelling hips.

She flushed angrily, unused to such rudely sexual attention.

Accepting the key without thanks, she marched haughtily across the floor to the elevator, stopping on the way at the news stand, to buy a newspaper.

The elevator took her up to her floor, where she stepped off and went down the dusky hall to her room. A pungent odor hung in the hall, too. Urine? Perhaps. Chipped paint flaked from the woodwork and, here and there, a loose end of wallpaper curled away from the wall. Probably, any hotel she could afford would be the same. Oh well, it was only for a couple of days... she hoped.

In her room, she gratefully put down the two heavy suitcases and looked around. The room appeared clean, but worn and drab. Certainly, it was no palace. So far, the city was a terrible disappointment.

Tomorrow she must find work, then an apartment. There were no other options. She almost wished that she had thought harder about Clyde's proposal, before turning it down.

Tears prickled. She brushed angrily at her eyes. I'm *not* going to cry, she vowed, biting furiously at her lip. Picking up the paper, she turned to the classified section.

"Here we are, help wanted," she murmured.

Treacherously, her eyes filled with tears. The news-paper blurred and she flung herself down across the bed, sobbing angrily, disgusted with herself and forlorn.

By an effort of will, she sprang up, washed her face with cold water, and forced herself back to the paper. She went through it carefully, marking any jobs she thought she might be qualified for. Then she planned her next day by plotting the job locations on a map of the city.

Finding work was not easy. "Any prior experience?" The question became the bane of her existence.

Even though she had taken office skills in high-school, typing, filing, office procedures, adding machine operation, she had no experience. Besides, it seemed that the offices were all computerized now and wanted someone with computer experience.

How could a person ever get experience? It was impossible, she decided, to get that first job that would give experience. You can't get a job without experience, yet you can't get experience without a job.

Perhaps she could get a factory job, she thought. She stood in line after line. The rain clouds had passed. For once, the wind had let up. It was hot and humid, midsummer. Perversely, she longed for a breath of cooling breeze.

A week had gone. Soon she would be out of money, she worried, and then what would happen to her? Maybe she should have married Clyde. He would be good to her.

Resolutely, she suppressed the urge to call him.

She stood in more lines. At the end of one, a kindly pair of eyes looked at her. He saw a young girl, slight and rather pretty, with amber, honey colored hair worn in a flowing angel wings style and enormous green eyes that looked haunted and desperate.

Orphaned, he saw in her application. Too bad. She rather reminded him of his own daughter. He wished that she were qualified for the job.

Oh, to hell with it. Take a chance, he thought, she looks sharp enough to learn and she certainly needs a break.

"Ok, kid," he said. "I have a trainee position. Six dollars an hour. Do you want it?" He saw the wave of relief wash across her features.

She could have kissed him, shouted out and danced for joy. Instead, she controlled herself and replied, "Yes, sir, thank you," with all the dignity she could muster.

The personnel man pushed a button. "Irene," he said, to the older woman who appeared, "I have a new trainee to work with Maggie. Please take her in and introduce her."

Turning to Elizabeth, he said, "The day is nearly over. Go meet Maggie. You start work at eight tomorrow morning."

He watched her go, feeling the warm glow of a good deed done.

She followed Irene out into a vast bay, filled with a roar of sound and smells of machine oil. They approached a girl who was taking up ornate left hand drawer handles from a bin and bolting them to each drawer of a series of dressers, as they moved slowly past.

"This is Maggie," said Irene, speaking loudly to be heard over the noises of the machinery. "Maggie, new girl to train with you." She turned and walked away.

Vivid orange-red hair and equally vivid blue eyes dominated Maggie's freckled face. She examined Elizabeth for several tense moments, then grinned.

She held out her hand. "Hi, like the lady said, my name's Maggie. What's yours?"

"Elizabeth Anne," she replied, taking Maggie's hand. Instinctively, she liked Maggie.

"Elizabeth Anne?" Maggie exclaimed. "God awful! They'll rag you terrible." She thought a moment, then proclaimed, "Your name is *Annie*."

"Annie" laughed. "Well, that's better than Lizzie, I guess." She almost felt like a different person. Somehow, she knew, an Annie was quite different than an Elizabeth Anne... better suited, perhaps, for making her way in the world.

A buzzer penetrated the din. The belt slowed to a stop.

"Quitting time," Maggie said, "Come on Annie, I'll buy you a beer."

Annie spluttered. Seeing Maggie looking at her questioningly, she said, "I've never drunk beer."

Maggie laughed, tossed her head, making her red curls bounce, and said, "Well, Hell! No time like the present to learn." She led the way out, stopping to insert a card in the time clock, then return it to the rack.

"You'll punch in here in the morning. The cards are kept in alphabetic order," she said and led on.

Halfway down the block stood another grimy, unprepossessing building. A neon sign flashed repeatedly *COLD BEER*. One *E* was burned out.

Maggie led Annie inside.

Inside, the tavern was cool and pleasant and, surprisingly, clean. A country western singer wailed from the juke box, a song of loss and sorrow. Blue clouds of tobacco smoke hazed the air and stung her eyes.

The clientele seemed a friendly lot. They greeted Maggie, who introduced Annie around. Most of them, she found, were fellow employees at the plant.

The malty, mildly bitter taste of the beer surprised and pleased her. She swallowed it thirstily and ordered another for herself and Maggie, recklessly spending her supper money. Oh well, now she had a job – she could splurge a little... Live it up.

As the waitress thumped the long neck bottles down on the table, another, wailing song began to play. A girl could get suicidal, listening to this stuff too long.

"Maggie, I need to find an apartment," she said. "Do you have any ideas?" She tipped up the bottle for another long swallow.

"Easy kid. That stuff'll do you in, if you aren't used to it," Maggie said.

"It's so good. The day has been a long, hot, dry one," said Annie, taking another swallow.

Maggie tipped back her bottle and drained it with several quick gulps.

She said, "I have a decent two-bedroom apartment and I just lost my roommate. She got married. Do you want to move in with me?"

Annie beamed with delight. She tilted the bottle and drained it. Already a little tipsy, she shouted, "Whoopee! I'd love that."

Grabbing her by the elbow, Maggie steadied her and said, "Well, come on, Kid. We'd better go move your stuff while you can still walk."

And so the friendship was born.Together, the girls laughed and played, worked and dated. For a time, life was good.

Winter came. The first snow fall. And there were snowballs in the park, and ice skating at the crowded rink. There were the museums and plays, fine deli's and cozy cafes.

The two friends roasted a turkey golden brown at Thanksgiving.

Christmas followed with its season of merriment. They rode the "El" elevated passenger train uptown to the loop, enjoying the festively decorated city sidewalks and department stores, bustling merry holiday crowds, bells and lights and fresh white snow.

Then, inevitably, city life began to pall for Annie. She was, after all, a country girl and aware of what was missing. Dreary January was followed by a drearier February and March. Frequent cold winds whistled off the lake.

The dirt and drabness, the bustling crowds and the incessant roar of traffic all began to take their toll.

The snow turned grey and slushy, then slowly dissolved. Finally, it was spring again in the city, then early summer. A year had passed quite quickly.

Annie slammed the apartment door behind her and threw herself disconsolately down onto the welcoming softness of her sofa. A soaking lock of hair straggled from beneath her water-logged hat.

She looked around the small, but elegantly furnished, apartment. It was expensive for working girls but worth it, an oasis of comfort and cleanness.

The blare of a horn on the street below was startlingly loud. Tires squealed, followed by the sound of crumpling fenders.

Moments later, angry shouts rose from four stories below.

She cringed, her nerves, already raw from the din in the factory, jumping at the continuing roar of traffic.

Restlessly she sprang up and moved to the window, stripping off her dripping hat and coat as she went. She flung the garments onto a chair and peered out.

Buildings, turned grey by years of smoke, dominated the view. The street was packed with its omnipresent traffic. Scurrying swarms of people packed the littered sidewalks.

The only greenery to be seen was a dispirited fern, drooping on the window sill. She had tried, God knows, talking to it, misting it with water, but, like her soul, it shriveled in the city atmosphere.

The sky carried through the dirty grey color scheme, an ugly drizzle dripping from the ashen clouds.

She turned, her attention caught by the sound of the door opening. Her roommate entered, disgustedly shaking water from her scarf.

Maggie carried the little bag of groceries that she had stopped for.

"Hi, Maggie," Annie said. "Nasty day." Her hazel eyes took in Maggie's state of dishevelment. A slight smile of amusement crossed her face.

Maggie strode across the room, throwing her coat on thc closet floor and grabbing a towel from inside the bathroom. "Annie, they are all nasty," she snapped, as she began to dry her dripping red hair.

Looking meditative, she continued, "The noise and dirt and crowds here in the city are driving me insane."

Maggie threw down the towel and began to run a comb through her unruly red locks. In the comb's wake, they sprang back in tangled, wet coils.

"I know what you mean," Annie replied. "I wish that I had found a way to stay in the country after my parents died."

She picked up Maggie's discarded towel and dried her flowing golden brown hair.

"Why didn't you try to run the farm?" Maggie asked.

At that, Annie's eyes snapped with indignation, appearing to change to green with her mood. The irises of her eyes were flecked green, brown, grey, blue and gold and seemed to change color depending on her mood, the lighting, or the color of her clothes. They were the best feature of her appearance, giving distinction to a face which would otherwise have been rather ordinary.

She took a deep breath before replying. Then she said, "Maggie, there was just too much debt. I couldn't have made it... not that I was offered the option. The banker was there like a vulture, before Dad and Mom were cold in their graves, with the foreclosure papers gripped in his talons."

Tears sparkled in her eyes, as she thought of the accident that had snatched her parents from her.

Impulsively, Maggie threw her arms around her friend, patting her shoulders.

Annie said, impatiently, "I'll be all right." She paused, blinking back the tears, then continued, "I almost wish I had married Clyde, from the neighboring farm. He offered, but he was just not for me, definitely bucolic – and a little too slow witted, the poor man. But he was nice. He would've loved me, though, and been good to me. Sometimes I wonder if that isn't all a girl dares to hope for."

Maggie sat down on the sofa. She shook her head, causing her red curls to bounce, and said, "He couldn't be any worse than what we meet here. They all seem to think of us as just another piece of meat and, besides sex, they have no interest in anything but television sports and beer... I just wish that I could meet a *real* man. I wouldn't give him even the faintest chance to get away." She wiggled her eyebrows wickedly, and grinned.

Annie sighed and appeared to droop. She nibbled absent mindedly at her lower lip, then responded, "Yes. There are two single women for every single man – and that's before eliminating the gays and the yuppie wimps. And just look at our job... boring, routine and dehumanizing. Life in the city kills the soul, maybe the mind, too."

Maggie jumped up and began to pace the floor, a flame kindling in her vivid blue eyes. "You're right!"she exclaimed, "I'm so damned tired of bolting the same left hand drawer handle onto the same drawers on the same dresser that I could scream." – Then she did, short and piercing, a real primal shriek.

"Hush!" Annie cautioned, "You'll have the neighbors calling the police."

"Why have we let ourselves fall into this rut?" Maggie asked. "Why don't we do something to change our lot?"

Annie looked at her warily and asked, "What are you thinking, Maggie?" She was used to following Maggie's lead, but this sounded dangerous.

A flush rose up Maggie's face. She replied, "Don't laugh, this is just a notion that crossed my mind, but think about it a minute."

Annie looked at her quizzically. Several moments passed in silence. "Well?" she said.

Maggie looked embarrassed but determined. "You know those magazines that I read?" she asked.

Annie said, "You mean those awful scandal magazines from the grocery store?" She felt distinctly skeptical now.

"Well... yes, but wait," Maggie answered, defensively. She paced another circuit of the small living room.

Then she continued, "They have a section of advertisements for mail-order brides. The ads are from all sorts of different places. I picked up this week's on the way home. I think we should consider them."

Maggie flushed beet red, as Annie burst into laughter.

Angrily, she said, "I told you not to laugh. After all, there might be a real prize of an honest, sincere, loving country man in those ads." She spread her hands in that ancient Celtic gesture that means "who knows?"

An indignant toss of her head set her curls to bouncing, again. "It would be an adventure," she argued.

Annie gulped down her laughter and controlled herself. She said, "I'm sorry, Maggie. We can look at the ads. It might be a fun way to spend a rainy Friday evening – Amusing, if nothing else." She shrugged and laughed. "But I don't have any great hopes for finding a treasure of a man from these ads. Maybe we could think about looking for jobs somewhere else, as an alternative."

Maggie grinned and said, "Thanks Annie. You're always a good sport. Maybe one way or another we can change our lives. It seems that we see so many people dragging along unhappily in a routine that they hate. And, yet, they never have the guts or imagination to make a change."

Annie giggled happily, caught up in mischievous Maggie's spirit of adventure. "I'll slip into my nightie and robe and make us some pop-corn and hot chocolate," she said. "It will be fun to think about."

The two friends, having changed into their nighties and robes, settled into the sofa. They munched popcorn and giggled over the ads. Maggie had equipped herself with a marking pen to circle any promising ones.

"Listen to this one," she said, and laughed, then read aloud, "Wanted, to share life and chores on busy chicken farm. Financially stable, attractive woman who enjoys housework, and farm chores. Must be a good cook, neat and clean."

"Oh, my," Annie said. "It sounds like he wants more of a cross between a slave and a mother than a wife. And financially stable, too." She chuckled.

She sipped her hot chocolate and turned the page. A bold heading caught her eye: "ALASKAN MEN," the advertisement read, "Two rugged manly men, warm and loving, aged mid-thirties, seek sensitive caring wives, age twenty-one to thirty-five, to share a fulfilling life in the wilderness. We are next door neighbors (only five miles apart). Photos and more detailed information available on request."

She pointed out the ad to Maggie, who placed a bold black circle around it. They read through the ads in all the magazines but no other ads caught their fancy. All the rest seemed good only for laughs. At the end, they returned to the ad placed by the "Alaskan Men."

It was Annie's turn to pace. She wrung her hands and cried out, "Oh, we can't just write to some strange men and send them our pictures."

"Damn right we can," Maggie replied. She looked in the mirror. Meditatively, she said, "I wonder if I should get my hair touched up and a new picture taken. I've always hated the carroty tone it has."

"That wouldn't be honest. Besides, your red hair and freckles are cute."

Annie paced some more. "I just don't know if I can do it. I have awful butterflies in my stomach, just from thinking about it. I'm such a coward."

"Well we can sleep on it," Maggie answered. "But don't turn chicken on me. Did you know that there are supposed to be three men for every woman in Alaska? They say that there are some real good catches running around loose up there."

In her room, Annie flicked off the bed side lamp and settled into her pillow in the soothing dark. Dreamily, she tried to picture life in the frozen arctic forests. As she drifted off to sleep, she dreamed of a bearded, fur clad giant.

The giant folded her into his embrace, then settled her into a dog sled, tucking furry robes about her. "Mush!" he roared at the team in a mighty voice. "Mush, you huskies."

She seemed to float as the sled glided off through the village of igloos and into the forest. Several times her mind pictured a bedroom with the bearded giant in it, but her imagination shied away from there.

Her giant offered her a heap of gleaming gold nuggets but, as she reached for them, a raging polar bear rose to devour her. A pack of ravening wolves circled, waiting for the remnants of her flesh, while some sort of buzzards circled and landed in the trees.

Annie woke with a shriek, the polar bear's snarls ringing in her ears. Grey morning light was filtering in around the shade and she was soaked with sweat.

Shakily, she recalled that it was Saturday morning and stretched, then snuggled into her covers. What ridiculous dreams, she thought. The whole idea is foolish anyway.

Resolved to sleep longer, she rolled over and closed her eyes but the effort was in vain. The rich smell of freshly perked coffee drifted in her door, accompanied in a short while by the aroma of maple cured bacon frying. Her watering mouth brought her out of bed.

She groped for her robe and, donning it, walked languidly out into the kitchen and peered out the window at the rain falling from the grey skies, soaking the grey buildings and the grey streets. And the roar of traffic continued. It roared twenty four hours a day.

Maggie looked at her and laughed. "Well good morning, sleepy head," she said. "Breakfast is nearly ready. – or should I say good afternoon?"

Annie, grunted, gratefully accepted the steaming cup of coffee that Maggie proffered, sipped at it, and sighed in contentment. "Well, what shall we do with the day?" she asked, adding, "It looks like a nasty day to go out, don't you think?"

"Annie!" Maggie exclaimed, with a toss of her head, her red curls bouncing, "Have you already forgotten that we resolved to do something to change our lives?" Her tone was reproachful.

As she turned the bacon and potatoes and broke eggs into the hot grease, they sizzled appetizingly. Unfortunately, Annie decided, she appeared to be quite in earnest.

Annie took another sip of coffee and felt rather distressed. Reluctantly, she said, "You mean it! You really want to write to those strange men and send our pictures, don't you?"

The frying eggs sputtered and popped. Maggie deftly flipped them over and said, "Oh, come on, Annie, it can't hurt. Then I thought that we could run to the book shop on the corner and get a book on Alaska and one on jobs in exotic places. Maybe we can send out some applications."

She dished breakfast up on two plates and thumped them down on the table.

Annie felt sulky, her lower lip protruding slightly, against her will. "You're so bossy," she muttered.

Maggie studied her and said, "If we don't do something, we'll still be here ten years from now... still hating the city and our jobs. Remember old Jenny? How she took early retirement and was going to do all the things she had put off."

After looking downcast a moment, she added, reflectively, "She died a month later of a heart attack – and never did any of them."

Her eyes flashed, as she recovered her natural exuberance and said, "Just think of the possibilities. Husbands in Alaska or a job at a resort in Hawaii, or an oil camp in Arabia – with all those handsome sheiks around, or jobs on a cruise ship to Bermuda, or maybe on a dude ranch in Wyoming."

Annie was, again, caught up in her friend's animated excitement. "Ok," she said. "Let's look at all the possibilities. It can't hurt to dream a little."

Her fork flew, as the two made haste to polish off their breakfast and get started on their adventures.

"Maggie," Annie said, as she cleared the table and began to wash the dishes, "We've got those pictures of us that were taken at the company Christmas party last winter. Do you think that they would do?"

"Hmmm, just maybe," the redhead replied. She rose, saying, "Let me find them."

Maggie began to rummage through the desk drawers.

Annie finished the dishes, thinking of the Alaskan Men as she worked. I wonder if he is kind and considerate. I suppose that it would be too much, to hope for him to be handsome, too, and maybe have a little money.

Her thoughts broke off, as Maggie bounced into the room, waving the pictures and exclaiming, "I think that these will be fine. They're pretty good and we are wearing our best outfits."

Annie sat at the table, taking the pictures from Maggie. She studied the picture of herself critically.

A young girl looked back at her, hardly more than a teen-ager in appearance. The deep green gown elicited a lovely green glow from her pictured eyes and set off her honey brown hair well.

She gasped at the amount of shoulder and neck displayed. She hadn't recalled that dress as being so revealing.

"Oh dear, Maggie, do you think that I look too immodest, almost ready for bed? I wouldn't want him to get the wrong idea."

A flush rose up her neck and face and her pulse raced as she imagined the impact of the picture on a strange man. The butterflies in her stomach were having a field day.

"You don't look like a hooker or anything," her friend reassured her, "and looking a little sexy can't possibly hurt your cause."

Maggie pretended to leer at Annie's picture and waggled her eyebrows comically.

"Oh!" Annie exclaimed. "That reminds me of those disgusting men down at the corner by the bar, arching their brows like that at the girls that pass by."

Maggie bubbled with laughter. "Exactly the impression I was trying to convey," she said. Turning serious, she asked, "What do you think about my picture?"

Annie looked at the picture of her friend. It was quite good. The peach gown seemed, surprisingly, to tone down and complement the orange red of Maggie's flowing shoulder length hair. With her vivid blue eyes and scattering of freckles, she was cute, as well as fresh and wholesome.

Annie said, "Well, you don't look like a hooker either." She paused and cocked her head, considering the picture.

"Well, thanks a lot, friend," retorted Maggie.

Annie laughed. Then she said, "I'm only joking. It's an excellent photo. I just wonder if we aren't both showing too much bare flesh, 'cause your gown even shows a bit of your upper breast."

Maggie frowned a moment at the picture, then said, "No. It's not showing enough to be immodest. Actually, we both look like innocent school girls instead of our true advanced ages."

Annie laughed and retorted, "I would hardly consider my twenty-three years to be an advanced age. Now you, at twenty-five, may be another matter."

Maggie snorted, then said, "It's settled then, we'll use these pictures." She tapped the pictures with her fore- finger and continued, "We may as well reply jointly, since the men advertised jointly."

Annie shivered and asked, "Oh, what are we going to say in the letter? This whole thing frightens me."

She reflected that Maggie was much the bolder of them and much better at coping with the city as a result. Maggie had also grown up on a farm, but had been in the city several years longer.

Maggie replied decisively, "I had better write for both of us. I don't want you to blow it."

"Oh, that's a relief!" Annie exclaimed. "But don't tell them any fibs."

Maggie laughed. "We'll go over it together, before I do the final version and mail it," she promised.

"I think that I'll clean house, while you work on the letter," said Annie. She took a cloth and a can of Pledge furniture polish from the cupboard. She hummed as she went into the living room.

Maggie got out paper and pen. She frowned as she considered what to say. Perhaps she should address the letter first, then just plunge right in. It was only a first draft, after all.

She wrote *Alaskan Men, C/O P.O. Box 51, Salchena, Alaska* ... she hesitated, uncertainly. "Annie," she called, "What country is Alaska in?"

Annie stopped her dusting and came back in. "I think it's part of the U.S... isn't it?" she answered.

"I thought that it might be," Maggie said, then giggled. "I guess that we'd better make that trip to the book store and learn a little more about Alaska before we try to write a letter."

Annie looked out the window at the continuing drizzle. She wrinkled her nose.

"Oh well," she said. "I guess that we can dash to the corner and back without getting too soaked." She brightened and said, "We haven't gotten to visit with Gramps recently anyhow."

The owner of the corner book store was affectionately known as Gramps to all of his regulars. His shop was somewhat of a social center, too, as well as a book store. To the girls he was almost like family, a spot of comfort in the impersonal city.

"Yes," said Maggie, "That'll be nice. And he may know something about Alaska."

Water ran from the girls' rain hats, as they burst through the door of their apartment. The visit with Gramps had been fun and they were laden with several books about Alaska. There were several more about jobs in exotic locations.

Gramps did, indeed, know of Alaska. He had spent two years there, thanks to the U.S. Army. His remarks were sobering. On the one hand, he confirmed the scarcity of women. He commented that they were prized. And treated better there, as a result.

On the other hand, he spoke of winter temperatures of sixty and seventy degrees below zero, and of forest cabins that many of the men lived in, with no running water or electricity.

They skimmed the books in fascination, exclaiming over dramatic photos and unusual facts.

After some time, Maggie leaned back, stretched, and shoved the books away. "Well," she said, "We did learn that Alaska is part of the U.S., however unwillingly. I think that I'll go ahead and write the letter. We will have time to finish reading the books while we're waiting for an answer."

"It sounds as though it could be a pretty grim lifestyle," Annie objected.

Maggie looked determined, as she said, "We can judge that better when we receive their answer to our letter."

She picked up the pen, finished addressing the letter, and began work on the letter itself.

Nearly two hours went by before she called Annie. The draft of the letter was complete. Crumpled pages of rejected attempts littered the floor but Maggie beamed with satisfaction.

Annie pulled up a chair and took the proffered letter. Lowering her eyes to the page, she read:

Dear Alaskan Men,

We are two warm and loving young women, whose potential as wonderful wives has gone unfulfilled in this metropolis. Single women here outnumber single men of marriageable age nearly two to one and most of the single men seem lacking by country girls' standards.

Both of us were raised on farms in the Midwest and yearn to return to rural life. The crowds and grime and noise of the city oppress our naturally sunny dispositions.

We remember the satisfaction our mothers took in their shelves of home canned goods, in their baking, and in the other visible accomplishments of their industry. We seek similar opportunity for ourselves.

What we seek is the same as what we offer — Love, respect, companionship and, in due time, babies to carry on after we are gone.

Our pictures are enclosed. They were taken when we were wearing our best dresses for the company Christmas party last winter.

Maggie (I am the red haired one) is twenty-five. I have a music keyboard, which I play fairly well. I like to read, dance to waltz music, and enjoy the outdoors. It would please me if I could learn some snow sports and to fish and hunt.

Annie (with the honey brown hair) is twenty three. I have similar interests to Maggie's. She is teaching me to play her keyboard. I have learned to waltz but do it rarely because I am shy with strange men. I would like to dance with my husband. I, too, would like to learn more outdoor activities.

Neither of us has been married. We look forward to receiving more information from you and your pictures.

Sincerely, Maggie and Annie

Annie looked up with gleaming eyes. "That's wonderful," she said.

"I think that they'll at least answer it, Annie," Maggie replied. "Shall I write that as the final draft, then, and mail it downstairs?"

"Yes. Do," Annie said. "What a change in our lives this would be. I feel frightened, don't you?" She nibbled her lower lip.

Maggie nodded and answered, "Yes, a little. Bear up though. It's not etched in stone, yet. And they may not want us, you know."

That night, Annie settled into her bed and attempted to read her latest favorite poetry book, a collection of Japanese Haiku. Failing to find peace in it, she turned to today's purchase – a book of Robert Service's Alaskan poems.

Caught up in the rhythms and imagery, she was swept away, reading on for over an hour. At last, feeling sleepy, she noted that it was well after midnight, turned out the light, and dreamed again... strange dreams of Alaska.

Ten days sped by, as the girls pursued their normal routine. The ten days grew to two weeks. Every day they checked their mail excitedly, looking for a letter from Alaska. Would it never come?

CHAPTER TWO

In Interior Alaska, it was a hot July day, a Saturday – but, of course, that makes no difference in the Bush. For, here, clocks and calendars lack the importance given them by urban dwellers.

A four-wheel-drive pickup truck pulled off the two-lane asphalt road, the northern extension of the Alaska Highway, running from Tok and Delta Junction on to Fairbanks. Stirring a cloud of dust, it drove up to a rough-looking old building. Built of logs, the building had served as a roadhouse during the gold rush days of the early nineteen hundreds.

A late model Ford, candy apple red, the truck looked sharp and well cared for. The driver, Kent Winfield, flung open the door, slid from the seat and, standing in the graveled parking lot, he wiped sweat from his bronzed face with a faded red bandanna. He stuffed a corner of the bandanna back into a pocket of his faded blue jeans.

A glance at the sun, blazing in the middle of the sky, confirmed that it was nearly noon. But that made no difference either, since it is light twenty-four hours a day during the Alaskan summer. The sun would near the western horizon, in due course, then slide in a vast circle along the northern horizon, to rise again in the north east.

Kent's hair, normally brown, was bleached blonde from the summer sun. Chocolate brown eyes peered intently out from beneath the brim of his stetson.

The jeans shirt, its arms ripped off, revealed muscular bronzed arms – the left one carrying tatoos from his special forces days. The tatoo on his upper arm, a screaming eagle with a snake clutched in its talons, bore the legend "Don't tread on me." Below it, on his forearm, slunk a sinister looking black panther, its open mouth showing formidible fangs. But those days were behind him, had been for some time.

The lot was empty, silent. Heat shimmered from the gravel. There was no sign of life, except for a dog sleeping by the door. The dog looked like it was part wolf. And it probably was, though no one knew

SALCHENA ALASKA
POST OFFICE

for sure.

A sign over the door read *Salchena Alaska – Post Office.* The post office stood next to the highway in the midst of a forest of mixed spruce and birch.

Dozens of white blooms of some wildflower mingled in the underbrush with yellow daisies and blue lupine. He couldn't remember the name just now, though it looked similar to lilly of the valley. Red fireweed fringed the edge of the clearing.

There was no town. The post office served scattered farms along the road and trappers, miners and other residents of the surrounding bush.

Kent strode up to the door, pausing to note that the thermometer beside it read eighty-nine degrees. It hung in the shade. He laughed again, seeing that the range ran only from minus eighty to plus one hundred twenty... not quite cold enough for the coldest days of some winters and not quite hot enough for the afternoon sun of the hottest summer days.

Official record cold, many places in Alaska, was only minus eighty, because that was all the colder the official thermometers would read.

He'd have to see about getting Robin a good thermometer.

He entered, walked to box 51, and opened it with his key. Startled, he jumped back, as a cascade of mail spilled from the opened door all over the floor.

Shaking his head ruefully, he laughed at himself, as he bent to gather up the mail.

From the back of the building he heard a stirring and looked up in time to see a plump grey-haired woman emerge. She leaned over the counter, looking at Kent's mail scattered across the floor.

"Why hello there, Kent," she greeted, a friendly smile on her face, "I've got lots more mail behind the counter for you and Blaine... a big carton full. It wouldn't all fit in the box."

She reached down and brought up a cardboard banana box full of envelopes, some pink or blue... even, a few, floral patterned.

With a knowing smile, she said, "It's mighty interesting mail, addressed in feminine handwriting, and smelling of perfume... nearly gave the old sled dog fits with all those different musk smells." She scanned him with sharp eyes, obviously wondering what explanation he would give.

He blushed. "Well, I reckon you caught us, Robin," he admitted, sheepishly. "Just like a bear with his head stuck in the honey pot."

"Look at you, Kent Winfield, you look just like a naughty little school boy. And coming on with those old 'down home' sayings," the postmaster declared – and laughed, a cackling laugh. Then she asked, "What exactly did I catch you at?"

He grinned easily, though he felt his ears still burning red, and said, "Well, it's this way. Blaine and I decided that we needed wives. But women are kind of scarce around these parts, unattached ones, anyway, so we decided to advertise in those scandal magazines... you know... like they sell at the grocery store."

Kent fidgeted with his feet, kicking at the floor with one toe of his scuffed engineer boots. At the moment, he did look very much like a naughty little school boy, caught at some prank.

"Ho ho ho," Robin laughed. "So you boys are going to get married. Well, it's about time, I must say. There are a couple of lucky girls out there somewhere."

Turning serious, she said, "Now, you boys want to be careful about who you pick out of these letters from would be mail-order brides. A certain number of them are likely to have either personality defects or problems with drink or dope."

"I know, Robin," he replied earnestly, as he bent and continued to pick up his scattered mail, "but we just didn't know how else to go about it. So, we tried this."

He gathered up more of the mail, then looked up and added, "Then too, I reckon that there'll be a good many that would be unable to stand the seclusion and the wilderness. We'll be careful, for we want to make good marriages."

With a smile of almost motherly approbation, she said, "Ok, then, good luck... Do you want my Old Man to bring anything from town for you before you come next week?" she added, as an afterthought, it seemed.

"No, but thanks. We'll be going in for winter supplies in a few weeks," Kent answered. He put the rest of his mail on top of the box, picked it up, and turned to leave.

"So long. Either Blaine or I will see you in a week, or so," he said over his shoulder, and closed the door.

Although his fingers itched to open the letters, he controlled his curiosity, reasoning that it was only fair to wait until he reached Blaine's place to look at the letters.

A short way down the highway, he turned his truck onto a narrow dirt road, just a pair of wheel tracks through the forest, really. He stopped a moment to put the truck into four wheel drive. Progress slowed to ten miles an hour, as he bumped along the ruts, willow brush and tree limbs scraping the truck on either side.

Never the less, the remaining eight miles to Blaine's seemed to go by swiftly, although a lazy cow moose blocking the trail made it necessary to stop at one point. There was no feasible way around her. In response to impatient honks of the horn, the moose ambled off the track.

It turned to glare in indignation as the truck went by and Kent laughed in delight.

The last mile of the drive was through their Christmas tree farm. His eyes swept the trees. They looked good.

He reflected on all the work that had gone into development of the tree farm, hard work. This was the oldest section and would be ready to harvest in only one more year. They were a pretty tree, given adequate spacing to grow properly.

They had set out a section each year for the last ten years. Next year they could begin selling trees for the Alaska market on a sustained yield basis. That would be a nice supplement to their other income.

Perhaps they could even make enough to, eventually, get away from their grueling midwinter stints in the North Slope oil fields, he thought.

He shivered, remembering the cold and the wind... often, wind chill factors to a hundred and twenty below zero.

Water sprayed as Kent's truck splashed across the ford of Blaine's Creek and into the packed earth clearing before Blaine's cabin.

Blaine had named the small creek himself since, like many things in this country, no one had ever gotten around to naming it before.

He tooted the horn exuberantly, as he skidded to a stop at the front door.

Blaine sauntered around the cabin, dressed in a pair of shorts made from cut-off jeans, a fringe of loose strings flapping at the bottom. His coal black hair topped a face and body that were swarthy from the burning summer sun of Alaska.

"Anything exciting in the mail?" Blaine called, his black eyes shining with anticipation.

Kent leaped from the truck and flourished the box of mail.

"Just look at this," he shouted and thrust the battered carton under Blaine's nose. "Just smell it, too. Smells just like a fancy New Orleans cat house."

Blaine threw up his hands. "I never in my wildest dreams expected a response to our ad like this!" he exclaimed.

"Let's sit down here on this bench in the sun and go through the mail," proposed Kent.

"You bet, old buddy," Blaine agreed. "Let's each keep out the ones that strike us as best."

The two friends basked in the sun and eagerly tore into the envelopes. As many letters as there were, going through them was a time-consuming venture.

Kent had one envelope that he was carefully saving to one side. A secret grin lingered on his face, but his partner's face grew long as the pile of rejected letters grew high.

Blaine threw down the last envelope disgustedly. He said, "None. There were letters from ladies in their fifties, letters from obvious city slickers, some from poor unfortunates that are horribly ugly – and our mention of wilderness lifestyle was a mistake... our ad brought out all the lunatic hippies and eco-freaks."

He glanced at Kent and caught the grin on his face. "Ah ha!" he exclaimed, snatching for the envelope. "Holding out on me, I see."

Kent danced away, holding the envelope tantalizingly out of reach. "Ah, ah, ah. Remember your manners," he said.

A joyous scuffle ensued, but Kent again danced out of reach, waving the envelope.

Finally, he relented and handed Blaine two pictures. With a flourish, he again unfolded the letter and read it aloud.

When Kent finished the letter and looked at Blaine, he found him staring spellbound at the pictures.

Blaine said fervently, "Wowee! A farm girl, and the right age, and she sounds like she would like the life here. On top of everything else, she is really cute."

"She sure is," Kent agreed heartily. "Look at that beautiful honey brown hair – and the glow in those green eyes."

"What? Brown hair?" Blaine exclaimed. "Oh, she's cute enough, I suppose, but it's the red-head that is the real looker."

Kent burst into laughter, pounding Blaine on the back, all the while.

Blaine glared at him, and demanded, "What in *hell* are you laughing at, you jackass?"

Kent sputtered a few moments longer, then said, "That's a real relief. I was wondering if I was going to have to fight you for Annie."

Blaine looked taken aback, then began to chuckle. "I see the light!" he declared. "It certainly is a good thing that we don't both want the same one, and it's nice for us that they are already friends, too."

"We may be getting ahead of ourselves, though," Kent said more seriously. "We need to send them our pictures and write them a letter explaining all about our life here."

"That's right, partner. We want to be sure that they know what they are getting into here. Too many women hate it here, in Alaska, and the next thing that you know they have run off back to America. You remember what happened to Siwash Pete over on Mud Creek?"

"Yeah. Brought in that fancy woman from New York. Not only did she hate the place and refuse to help with the chores, but she pinched his poke of gold and caught a plane back outside – disappeared – he never saw her again. Left him broke and broken hearted... both."

"Well, no time like the present. We'll be frank about life here... Let's each sit down and write a letter to our girl," Kent replied. He carried the mail into the cabin, gathered up writing materials, and propped Annie's picture up before him on the table.

He studied the picture for some time and carefully reread the letter.

While reading, he absently fingered the heavy scar that ran diagonally across his left cheek. The guerilla's machete slash had, long since, ceased to trouble him but fingering the scar had become an ingrained habit. His fingers strayed to the angry scar, high on the left side of his chest, absent mindedly stroking it, too.

For a time, he became lost in thought, his mood gradually changing from bright to sombre. Then his face crumpled. A faint sob caught his friend's attention.

"Blaine," he said, seeing his friend gazing at him, "this here might've been a mistake, our sending for brides."

"Si, senor." Blaine replied, in a soft drawl, as he looked into Kent's eyes and at the tremors shaking his frame. "Ah-huh, Old Buddy, you're recalling Juanita, down there in the jungles. Sweet little Juanita – round, soft and warm. But she's gone, long gone – cold in the ground twelve years, or more."

There was a far away look in Kent's eyes. "Yeah. I thought I was in love... *Hell*! I was in love. Then the damn little bitch led me into an ambush." He could hear the bitterness in his own choked voice. "Yeah, Captain Winfield – hot shot platoon leader."

Sweat bathed his face.

A sudden, waking nightmare seized him. Bright orange tracer fire, a string of explosions in the night, screams of agony and the wheezing, slobbering sobs of someone shot through the lungs – burned into his mind – a betrayal he could never forget. Streaks of orange fire burned, again, across the darkness... jungle rain wet his face, or was it tears? The whole platoon, dead, because he had trusted her... There had been the soft voice, the lifted brow, the flashing midnight eyes in a face framed by midnight hair and, at last, the soft yielding inside his sleeping bag – the miracle, the gift of herself. And he had trusted her.

And they had all died.

Blaine didn't understand, he'd brought his boys back – most of them.

"Kent! Kent!" Blaine's voice, full of alarm, and a stinging slap on his left cheek, snapped him out of it. Shamed, he realized that his body was racked with sobs, his face wet with tears.

"I'll be all right," he gasped, "Thought I was done with those nightmares... now I feel like a load has lifted, a heavy load I've carried all these years."

"We should have talked about it before," Blaine said, tensely, "but, God *damn* it, you would never let me even bring it up."

"I never could talk about it before.Talking about taking a wife brought it out – I had it buried deep. Maybe I needed to clear it up, before going on with my life," Kent muttered.

"She tried to save you at the end, you know, covered you with her own body after that crease across the skull finally put you down," Blaine said. "You were so limp and so covered with her blood and yours, that they must have thought you were dead. We found her that way – lying on top of you, cradling you, with her cheek next to yours. She'd been shot twice, undoubtedly bullets meant for you. I'm not so sure that she betrayed you... not deliberately."

"Aw, that'll take some of the horror out of the dreams, too." Tears rolled from his eyes, but without the bitter, racking sobs. "Pard, did we do the right thing, down there?"

"We thought so at the time. Our countrymen thought so, too, some of them."

"Yeah, and some of them didn't."

They pondered that in silence, remembering the Senate hearings, the news coverage.

"Phony bastards, living in a temporary pool of peace and security, created by the blood and suffering of better men than them, and deluding themselves that that's the real world. – Some things *are* worth fighting for and sometimes you have to fight. There are some truly evil men in the world."

"Yuppies!" Kent made a swear word of it. "Thank God, we came out here, got away from political correctness and all the phony bull shit and piles of regulations. I don't know how they can live like that."

"Well, I'll tell you, I did what I thought was right, Old Buddy, and I'm carrying no guilt over it. I'll tell you this, though, that I'm never fighting again in a foreign land. They come after me here, they'll get one hell of a fight, but no more damn jungles!" Blaine said it fiercely.

"Well, let's put it behind us. I wish now that we had talked this over several years ago. It seems to have laid the ghost. I'm going to be fine now."

With a sigh and a straightening of his broad shoulders, Kent took pen in hand and, again, applied himself to writing the letter.

Nearly an hour later, he looked up, his attention caught by the sound of crumpling paper. Blaine tossed another rejected attempt to the floor, to join a litter of previously rejected attempts.

He caught Kent's eyes upon him and laughed, ruefully. "I'm usually not at a loss for words," he said. "But this is different, though."

Kent eyed his own pile of crumpled paper and replied, "I think that I finally have one going that I'm going to be satisfied with. Maybe we should just write one letter to the girls, since most of what we want to tell them is the same. Then we can each add just a brief note to the one that we have picked out."

Blaine looked relieved. With a nod, he pushed back his chair and stretched to relieve the cramped muscles that had resulted from hunching over his writing.

"Ok, Kent," he said. "I'll get out my pictures and pick out some that I think might be good to send the girls." (They were both calling Maggie and Annie "the girls" by now.)

He rose, walked into his bedroom, and began rifling through his top dresser drawer.

Kent turned his attention back to the chore of writing the letter.

Now that his line of thought was established, his pen flew across the paper. He had just leaned back, at last, smiling with satisfaction, when Blaine returned with a few pictures he had selected.

Blaine glanced at the table in front of Kent and exclaimed, "By gosh, it looks like you wrote a book!"

"Only five pages," Kent retorted, with a laugh. "Read them and see what you think."

Blaine pulled up a chair, set down the pictures, and became immersed in the letter. A series of expressions played across his expressive face. Some passages elicited a smile, while others, here and there, caused a frown to appear briefly.

"Well, pard, you make it sound pretty rough here, in places. I guess that it's for the best, though, that they have a good idea of conditions here. We need to be honest. I'd hate to discourage them but we don't want them to get so disillusioned later that they run off, either."

Kent nodded, in agreement. "I reckoned that honesty was best," he said. His eyes turned to the pictures. "What photos have you picked out?" he asked.

Blaine silently handed him the pictures.

He nodded as he looked them over. Then he looked up at Blaine and said, "I like the one of us with our big moose and the one of us in the middle of building your new shop building best. Let's just send all these though."

Blaine nodded and reached for pen and paper. "I'll just write my note to Maggie now," he said.

Kent, too, applied himself to his personal note to Annie. His mind was already made up... the letter ended with a proposal of marriage and a request that she set a date so that he could send her an airplane ticket. In this letter, he enclosed a picture of himself in swimming trunks, taken down by Blaine's creek. The photo made it obvious that he was bronzed all over. He leaned back, grinning with satisfaction. The packet was a good one, the letters and pictures. The priority task of the day accomplished, he recollected the other paper in his pocket. He took it out and handed it to Blaine.

"Here old buddy. I brought this along, too. It's a copy of my latest poem."

Blaine bent his head over the sheet and read it aloud:

"WHEN DOES THE FUN START?

Dreary, dark, dismal, dripping,
from sullen brooding skies;
daunting, drenching, steady rain,
upon the foliage sighs.
From each leaf, each tree and bush,
damp, dank drizzles drain.
Grim, grey, gulches gushing rain,
rain puddles on the flat,
mushy, moldy, squishy moss,
and on the creek, a steady splat.
I travel on, a plodding pace,
I really feel like heck.
I brush the water from my face,
it's dripping down my neck.
Dripping, draining, from my hat,
it's dampening my shirt.
Pants seat wet, where I sat,
when I fell on slippery dirt;
pants legs, wet from dripping brush,
are stuffed in rain filled boots.
We came out on this camping trip,
in the land of midnight sun.
I trudge on through the steady drip,
Now we're having fun!"

A broad grin broke out on his face and he chuckled heartily. "Well, I'll be darned if you haven't captured the exact flavor of our prospecting trip last month. And, I reckon, the sourdough attitude. Sure, that poem would strike a true note with any outdoorsman around here, since the catch word when everything goes to shit is 'Remind me of how much fun we're having.' or 'When does the fun start?' I've heard them both a hundred times."

"I'll add it to my collection. Old Buddy, why don't you send these in to a publisher, or one of those contests? I think your poems are good enough to make it – though your first ones, about the fighting, made my blood run cold."

Kent was shaking his head, a frown on his face. "No, they started out as self-prescribed therapy. Now they are just something I do for fun."

"Chicken?" Blaine taunted.

"Well, maybe so. I don't want to have them rejected, and prove that they're not good enough. I'd rather keep on treasuring them and thinking that they're good."

"I'm certain they're good enough." Changing the subject abruptly, Blaine added, "Ready for some chow? I've got taco fixings and chili just about ready to eat."

"Aw, you know tacos are my weakness. Remember, back in high school, when we worked for Juan's Tucson Eats."

"Do I ever," Blaine drawled. "Fringe benefits was all the tacos we could eat." He laughed. "Remember how the tourists would order a chiliburger, thinking they was covered with mild American style chili. Most of 'em didn't look to see that layer of chopped green chili peppers, just the way the Mexicans like 'em – oh my, tears in their eyes, and they'd down a coke in one gulp. I reckon it was mean, but it sure seemed funny, at the time. – We sold a lot of coke refills that way, too."

Blaine had been setting the table, while he talked, and a silence fell as the men concentrated on the food.

At length, Kent groaned and patted his belly. "No more, pard, I think I'd explode... and it'd be a hell of a mess."

He shoved back the chair, rose, and sauntered to the door. Looking out, he saw that the sun was barely above the western horizon. It was getting late and he had five more miles of narrow trail to travel on his three wheeler. The truck could go no further.

"I reckon that I'd better get on my way, pardner," he drawled.

"Judging by the sun, it must be nearly midnight."

Blaine dug out his pocket watch and looked at it. "You're right. It's eleven thirty-four," he said.

He inserted his letter to Maggie into an envelope. "I'll run down to the post office tomorrow and mail our letters," he said.

Kent grinned. "Come on up and see me in a week or so," he invited. "We can barbecue some moose steaks and suck up a couple of drinks." He had walked out and mounted his three wheeler while he was talking.

"I'll be there," Blaine replied, standing in the door. He lifted his hand in a casual wave, as Kent started across the yard toward the Winfield Trail.

Kent briefly returned the wave, then turned his attention to riding. The trip up the five miles of trail required attention and skill.

As the vehicle bounced and lurched, Kent held on tightly, shifting his weight back and forth to help control the direction of the machine.

There was no need to worry about being caught in the dark, for this was still the time of year that it never got fully dark.

For a week, around June twenty-first, the sun never set at all. From then until December twenty-first, when the sun barely cleared the southern horizon, daylight was lost at an average seven minutes a day.

In December Alaskans got only a few hours of dusky twilight.

Kent savored the magical golden glow in the summer sky and the scents of the summer forest.

At a muddy spot in the trail, huge bear tracks oozed water freshly, prompting Kent to feel for his pistol and assure himself that it was still there. Fervently, he hoped not to run across that bear. It looked to be an almighty big grizzly, though no bear, even a small blackie, was to be taken lightly.

Momentarily, his memory was haunted by the girl who had lost both arms, eaten off by a grizzly bear on the upper Salchena, and by the others, over the years, killed or maimed by the big bears. In Alaska, there were four or five people killed every year by the bears... sometimes more. The hair on the back of his neck prickled uneasily.

At last, the three-wheeler splashed across another creek, wide but shallow, and in another half mile he was home.

Upon finally reaching home, he dug out Annie's photograph and studied it fondly, before entering the cabin. She sure is a beauty, he mused. A fantasy of her floated in his mind, warm, feminine and tender in his bed. He studied the sky, stroking the scar that angled across his cheek, and noted that just the upper disc of the sun was showing above the hills to the northeast, having slid on around the northern sky while he traveled.

"Ah huh," he grunted. "Nearly time for sunrise." He slapped at an overly aggressive mosquito... his repellent must be wearing off. The usual cloud of mosquitos hovered nearby.

Peach colored clouds dusted the hill tops. It was one a.m. The garden caught his attention and he crossed the yard to inspect it.

The long rows of potato vines were flourishing, their flower buds beginning to open into purple blooms. As he moved down the rows, everything looked healthy, lettuce, radishes, carrots, turnips, beets, green beans, and peas.

His few cabbage plants looked as though they would already weigh nearly forty pounds each. He hoped to get at least one large enough to enter in the fair, but they would have to do considerable growing yet. It wouldn't be worth entering one less than a hundred pounds.

It was a big garden. Kent bought little at the grocery, growing and preserving most of his own vegetables and taking his meat, fish and fowl from the forest around him. He dried, he canned, he smoked, he pickled... His self-sufficiency was a matter of pride to him.

Amidst a sea of white blooms, lots of strawberries were ripe and he knelt beneath the midnight sun to gather a hat full. A strawberry short cake would go real good tomorrow – maybe, even, for breakfast.

Once inside, he stripped and went naked to bed, as was his custom. He was dreaming almost before he hit the pillow, Annie's face floating before him. Would she accept him?

A frown grew on his face. Would she adapt to this wilderness life, to him? Or would she run off?

CHAPTER THREE

Crowds of people thronged the city park, making the most of a sunny weekend.

Annie opened her mouth and popped in the last bite of her sausage. She chewed and swallowed with pleasure. The sourness of the kraut was a pleasing complement to the pungent spices of the knackwurst and the mustard.

"Mmmm," she sighed with contentment. "I'm stuffed."

She wriggled in the Saturday afternoon sunshine, where she and Maggie lounged on the park bench. The warmth was pleasant.

After a few moments of silence, though, a frown flickered across her face. She chewed her lower lip, reflectively.

Maggie noted the frown, and asked, "What's wrong Annie?" She sucked ketchup from her forefinger and wiped her hands with a paper napkin.

"Nothing, really," Annie replied. "It's just that I feel so hemmed in by all the people, constantly around all the time. It makes me feel a little crazy, kind of claustrophobic."

Maggie nodded. "Yes," she said, "There must be thousands of people here in the park. And the noise – kids yelling, traffic. And strange men staring – I do mean *strange*, too. I know exactly what you mean."

"Let's go back to the apartment. At least we have some privacy there and the noise is less," said Annie.

"We can swing by the deli on the way and pick up something exciting for dinner," Maggie exclaimed, as she jumped up.

"That'll be fun," She added, "We can get something sinful... and cheesecake for dessert... and some wine."

Annie stood up, smiling. "Thanks, Maggie. You always snap me out of it,"she said.

After a momentary pause, she continued, "Do you want to stop by the art museum on the way? I enjoy the pictures and it's a haven of quiet and peace."

She looked at Maggie and received a Gallic shrug and a grin.

"And why not?"Maggie asked, her hands spread wide and palms up.

They tossed the remnants of their lunch into a trash can and strolled away a short distance down an asphalt path to the edge of the park and the street that led to the museum.

Arriving at the curb just as the walk light flashed on, they stepped into the cross walk. They hurried across, caught up in the bustle of the crowds, but as they neared the far side of the street, the blare of a horn alerted them to the presence of an onrushing cab. It had rounded the corner, through the red light, and was bearing down on them rapidly, its horn continuing to blare.

The rest of the crowd scattered, dashing for safety, but Annie froze, her scream stifled in her throat. The cab grew, dominating her whole vision as it rapidly bore down on her. In her terror, she was unable to move.

"I'm going to die," she thought. "I should have gotten out of this horrible city sooner – now it's too late."

Dimly, she was aware of Maggie dragging her by the arm, out of the street and up the curb.

The wind of the passing cab ruffled her skirt.

"Stupid bitch!" the driver yelled, making an obscene gesture out the window, as his cab receded down the street.

Maggie returned the gesture, hoping that the bastard would see it in

TAXI

his rear view mirror. No use to get his license number, the cops wouldn't do anything. – Damn city drivers, especially the cabbies. She hugged Annie, who stood numbly, tears trickling down her cheeks.

The crowd pushed by impatiently, seemingly oblivious to the near miss. More likely, just not caring about it – calloused emotionally and mentally. Metropolitan living does that... destroys sensitivity.

"Don't cry, Annie," she said and patted her consolingly. "Here, take my hankie and dry your tears. We'll stop at that quiet little lounge by the museum and get a drink. You need one for your nerves."

She took the hankie, nodded, and dried her tears. Forcing a smile, she said, "Well, then, let's go on...Thanks, Maggie."

With an effort, she calmed herself slightly, as they walked the few blocks to the museum, although the repeated jostling she received from the rude herd did not help.

The lounge, as they entered, was a pool of tranquillity, cool and dark. Breathing a sigh of relief, they settled into the relative privacy of one of the high backed booths.

Snuggling into the security of the plush seat, Annie let the quiet piano music soothe her further. "That has to be one of Richard Clayderman's albums," she said. "He plays so wonderfully, that there's no mistaking his style."

"May I help you?" asked the waitress, who had unobtrusively appeared. Annie jerked, startled out of her reverie.

Maggie replied, "Yes, thanks, double scotch for both of us – straight up."

The scotch appeared in short order and Annie took the first sip, shuddering slightly at the faintly medicinal taste.

The girls sipped in silence, letting the music flow over them. Still unaccustomed to drinking, Annie felt the liquor spread a warm glow throughout her. It began to taste quite nice, smooth on the tongue.

"Well, Maggie," she said, "the Alaskan Men must not have been interested in us. It's getting on into August, the fifth already, and we've heard nothing from them."

She felt her mouth droop into a suggestion of a dispirited frown but lacked the will to put on an expression of good cheer. She sought further comfort in her glass and found some measure of it there. For the moment, at least.

Maggie sipped at her drink, studying her friend over the rim of the glass, then set her drink down and answered, "No. We haven't seen any other ads that we wanted to reply to either. Maybe we should look at our other options."

Annie sighed. "Too bad, I liked the sounds of the Alaska Men. But working someplace else does sound fun. We've gotten some response to those letters – job offers from two resorts in Hawaii, that ski resort in Colorado and the dude ranch in Arizona."

A tiny smile tugged at the corners of her mouth. "Well, those all sound pretty nice," she said, "At least for a consolation prize."

A big grin grew on Maggie's face and lit her blue eyes. She exclaimed, "They do sound nice and I'll bet there are some great men there. Let's do it!" Her eyes fairly snapped with an infectious enthusiasm.

Annie's reflective smile grew. "Ok," she agreed musingly. "We can make a decision tonight, mail off our answer tomorrow, and start buying plane tickets and packing."

Excitedly, Maggie flung money on the table and tossed down the rest of her drink. "Let's skip the museum," she cried impulsively and jumped up.

Annie was galvanized into action and thumped her glass down on the table, no longer interested in the whiskey.

She rose swiftly, saying, "Yes, let's blow our budget and splurge on some fancy hors d'oeuvres and wine at the deli, like it was New Year's Eve, or something, and go home to look over our books and brochures. We need to discuss our choice. One way or another, we'll get out of this damned city."

They hurried up the street, ignoring the jostling crowds as they excitedly discussed the possibilities.

"Visions of palm trees dance in my head," enthused Maggie. "And look at that blue surf crashing on the pure white sand."

Annie glanced at Maggie and saw a far away look in her eyes. "Maybe so," she said, "but so far as the men go, I think that I would prefer a rugged cowboy to a beach boy or ski bum."

Maggie appeared about to argue the point, but suddenly exclaimed, "Oh! Here's the deli. We nearly walked right by it."

Annie laughed. "We aren't excited, or anything, are we?" she exclaimed.

The next half hour was spent pleasurably, stocking up on delicacies for a celebration. Smoked ham and smoked turkey joined several fine cheeses in the basket, along with pickled artichoke hearts and mushrooms.

A real cheese cake and a bottle of Asti Spumante completed their purchases.

They chattered excitedly as they walked to their apartment, giggling girlishly.

"Here, hold this," Maggie said, handing her bag to Annie. She dug out her keys, and let them into the front door of their apartment building.

"I feel positively festive," she said, letting the door close behind them.

They crossed the lobby to the mail boxes, stopping to check their mail before going on up stairs.

Maggie inserted her key in the lock and opened the mail box. Pulling out a thin handful of mail, she flipped through it hopefully.

"Nothing here but ads," she said, smiling a forced looking smile. As they walked to the elevator, she added, "I had still hoped that there might be a letter from Alaska."

Annie nodded glumly.

The elevator stopped, announcing its presence with a ding. Just as Maggie and Annie stepped on, their gossip-loving landlady, Mrs. Schmidt, entered the building and boarded with them.

"Well what are you girls up to these days?" she asked, peering at them over the top of her bifocals.

"We just had a picnic in the park. It's such a lovely day," Annie replied evasively.

She saw no need to have their plans gossiped about to all the neighbors, until they had been firmed up.

Mrs. Schmidt nodded and said, "Yes, I do hope that you look out for sunburn. You want to be careful about that and be sure that you wear sun screen." The elevator stopped at their floor.

With relief, the two friends bade Mrs. Schmidt good evening and escaped into their apartment. The old busy-body.

"Ohhh!" said Annie, "I'll lay out our feast, while you get out our literature on the four resorts. Really, in spite of what I said, I think that I like the one at Hanalei best, though. I keep seeing that long curve of white beach, backed by forests of palms and those incredible ragged volcanic mountains. It just keeps popping up in my mind... It's where they filmed South Pacific, you know."

She busied herself with the deli bags and began to slice the meat and cheese and arrange it attractively on a platter.

A knock on the door brought Maggie hurrying back into the room. "I'll get it," she called.

As Annie sliced the rest of the meat and cheese, she heard the murmur of voices from the front door. She looked up curiously, when Maggie returned, and asked, "Who was it?"

Maggie flourished an envelope dramatically. "This," she proclaimed, "was put in the wrong mail box. Mr. Larson just brought it over."

"It isn't a letter from Alaska by any chance?"Annie asked, disbelievingly. She arranged the last of their snacks on a platter.

"Look and see for yourself," Maggie said, handing her the fat envelope. She looked at the table and continued, "My, that looks good. You have such a nice touch with food and decoration, you'll make some lucky man a great wife." Her right eyebrow shot up in an evil arch.

Annie took the envelope and felt her excitement rising as she read the return address, *Kent Winfield and Blaine Burns – Box 51, Salchena, Alaska.*

She held it a moment, looking at it, reluctant to break the spell by tearing it open. Her mind drifted off into pleasant fantasies about its contents.

"Well open it!" exclaimed Maggie. Her impatience was fueled by a sweet surge of blood coiling within her. Her curls bobbed in response to a toss of her head.

"Look at you! Already blushing like a bride, and we haven't even opened the letter," Annie said with a laugh.

Her fingers were busy, though, as she spoke. She picked up the knife that she had been using to slice the meat. With it, she slit the envelope and pulled out its contents.

"Me?" Maggie retorted. "You seem to have considerably more color than you did a few minutes ago. And look how your fingers are shaking."

Annie felt a new wave of heat burn across her cheeks.

The envelope had contained three more envelopes, one addressed to Annie, one addressed to Maggie, and one for both of them.

Annie's was addressed "To Annie from Kent Winfield."

With shaking hands, she handed Maggie's envelope to her and tore open her own. A picture dropped out as she extracted the folded pages. She picked it up and studied it.

He grinned at her boyishly from the photo, fine laugh wrinkles at the outer corners of his sparkling chocolate drop brown eyes. He appeared to be bursting with exuberant good humor and joie de vivre. Beneath close cropped brown hair, he had a good face, strong and square, with a firm chin.

His face is rugged and uneven, she thought, good looking, in a manly John Wayne sort of way. Certainly not pretty-handsome, as the fad is here.The jagged scar across his left cheek lent an air of intrigue, a piratical air.

She felt an odd melting sensation somewhere inside herself. "Kent," she said. "Kent Winfield... Annie Winfield," she tried the sound of it softly. It sounded good, but frightening.

In the picture, Kent was standing on the edge of a pond, wearing swimming trunks that appeared to be denim trousers with the legs cut off.

A subtle swell of muscles showed beneath a reddish-golden tan, well developed, but not to the point of deformity. Brown hair curled crisply on his chest.

Another long scar was visible on one of his muscular legs, the calves of which curved strongly and pleasingly with the swell of muscle. An odd, raggedly roundish scar stood out whitely against his tanned shoulder, upper chest, really – just below the left collar bone.

Viscious looking, a panther tatoo sneaked sinuously across his fore-arm, giving him a faintly disreputable air, like a biker. Yet he didn't look like a Hell's Angel otherwise, except, maybe, for the scars. Really, he looked very nice... just enough faint air of danger to make him intriguing.

Across the pool of water, behind Kent, a riot of pink roses showed against a background of evergreen trees.

Her heart was pounding, the blood singing in her ears and burning her cheeks, as she turned her attention to his letter, unfolding it with trembling fingers.

She read, *"My Darling Annie. I call you that because you captured my heart the moment I saw your picture, with the lively sparkle in your beautiful green eyes and your lovely honey-toned hair."*

"I can tell by your letter that you want the same things from life that I do — and I am sure that you will love my wilderness home. The longer letter, addressed to both of you, describes our wilderness lifestyle — both the good points and the draw-backs."

"After you read that letter and give it some hard thought, you would make me a very happy man if you consent to be my wife. If you agree, please write and let me know when you can come. I will send you a plane ticket immediately."

"It is my thought that we can have a small wedding at the Salchena Lodge and go to our home for a couple of months so that you can get to know me and your new home. Then we can continue the honey-moon with a month in Hawaii – I have a favorite resort there that

I'm sure you can't help but love. After our trip to Hawaii, we have to go to the Arctic Ocean, where Blaine and I work as consulting geologists from January first to March thirty-first each year. Does that plan please you?"

"They pay well for our three months of long hours in severe conditions, enough to be a year's living. The rest of the year we live in the Salchena River valley in the golden heart of Alaska, where we work on our tree farm, hunt, fish and garden and cut a little firewood for sale."

"It's a good life, close to God and nature and far removed from the stresses and throngs of the cities."

"Please reply favorably very soon. I can hardly stand the suspense."

"With highest regard, Kent"

Unshed tears of emotion sparkled in her eyes and her blood thundered in her ears, as she studied the picture of this man who proposed to change the entire course of her life.

Maggie's voice penetrated the mists. Annie looked up and said, "I'm sorry Maggie, what did you say?"

Maggie studied her and replied, "You've got it bad, Annie. You look positively radiant with those rosy cheeks and glistening eyes, just like a new bride."

Annie smiled, a little tremulously. She said, "You have a glow too, Maggie. Shall we read the other letter?" She reached out and picked it up. In response to Maggie's nod she unfolded it and read it aloud.

The reading over, the two girls sat silently a moment, mulling over the contents of the letter.

"Look," Annie said, "There are more pictures in the envelope."

Eagerly the friends spread out the pictures and pored over them. There were photos of two rustic log cabins, snow shoes, traps and rifles hanging from the walls. Another showed Kent and Blaine working with chain saws to build a new log building. There were pictures of the two with fish and, grinning proudly, with a huge dead moose. Other pictures showed the gardens and tree farm.

One showed a desolate-appearing wasteland, stretching flat and white into the distance, and a tiny-looking living unit. A sort of trailer, it appeared. Kent stood by the door, clad in bulky bundles of clothing, a large ruff of fur surrounding his face. This, the caption said, was winter camp near the Arctic Ocean – at 86 degrees below zero. There were no trees to be seen, no buildings to break the desolation, except, of course for the camp.

Another note was jotted at the bottom of the picture: *"The only good things we can say about this one are that the pay is excellent and it lasts only three months a year."*

Annie stood and walked to the window. She gazed out, then turned back to face Maggie.

"They are beautiful," Maggie breathed. "So masculine-looking and full of joy and life." Her face was rosy with feeling and her eyes, too, sparkled moistly.

Annie nodded mutely. An enormous lump in her throat seemed to block her words. Tears overflowed her eyes and ran down her cheeks.

With a cry she ran to Maggie and the two clung to each other, sobbing happily.

Annie gulped and sniffed. "I'm just crying because I feel so happy," she explained. "Kent asked me to marry him."

"And Blaine asked me," Maggie confided softly.

The girls separated, gazing at each other wonderingly.

"Maggie!" Annie exclaimed, "I had thought... well, that we would probably write letters back and forth and meet sometime, before marriage was mentioned... but... I'm going to say yes. They seem so nice! I want to do this. But I'm *so* scared." She was pale with emotion and breathless.

After a pause, Annie controlled herself, gulped at the lump in her throat, and continued, "I hope that you're going to marry Blaine. It'll be less frightening going to a new husband in the wilderness, if you are going to be my neighbor." Annie looked at her hopefully.

Maggie's red curls bounced as she tossed her head and laughed. "Of course I'm going to marry him," she proclaimed confidently. "I'm going to write back this evening and accept. He isn't going to get even the slightest chance to reconsider, because I plan to settle down and make lots of little red-headed, freckled, Alaskan babies."

Annie smiled. "Let's eat our celebration dinner, while we talk about what we're going to say and figure out our plans. We've changed what we're celebrating, but it still is one." She sat at the table and applied herself to opening the wine.

Maggie pulled up a chair and sat at the table. She looked thoughtful, as she popped a pickled artichoke heart into her mouth and reached for a cube of smoked turkey.

She said, "Well, by contract, we have to give four weeks notice at work, or we lose two weeks' pay. And then we need time to do some shopping and to pack."

"Oh, damn!" Annie exclaimed.

"What?" A red eyebrow arched questioningly.

"This darned cork crumbled on me. I never have been able to open wine bottles right." She took a table knife and shoved the remnants of the cork into the bottle, then poured the sparkling wine into the glasses, while holding the cork below the neck with her knife.

"There's only a few crumbs of cork in it," she said, defensively. She lifted hers and sipped it appreciatively.

"Mmmm!" she said, "That is good wine. – We have to give a month's notice that we're moving out of here too, so we'll be paying rent to September 30."

Maggie took a sip of her wine and nibbled at a bit of delicate cheese. Contemplatively, she said, "Well let's see. It's August fifth. Couldn't we be ready to leave by the fifteenth of September?"

As Annie finished chewing and swallowed her piece of tangy cheddar, she nodded, then said, apprehensively, "What if I don't please him, Maggie? I've never been to bed with a man and don't know what to do."

Her cheeks were burning, hot with a furious blush.

Maggie laughed. She replied, "Be calm, Annie. Just tell him. I'm sure that Kent will be pleased – and proud to teach you."

Maggie topped off their glasses. Lifting hers high, she proclaimed, "A toast. To our marriages, may they be long and happy. And to our new life in Alaska."

Annie lifted her glass, clinking it against Maggie's. "And to two real men," she added.

Maggie giggled. In response to Annie's questioning look, she explained, "It didn't take us long to forget Hawaii and the beach boys... and your rugged cowboys, too."

They looked a moment at each other and burst into gales of silly laughter, frivolous and happy.

Eventually the celebration was over, the food eaten and the wine drunk.

As Annie began to clear the table, Maggie leapt from her chair, saying, "Now I'll go get the stationery and envelopes. We can get our letters to Kent and Blaine in the mail this evening."

"Perhaps we should wait until we're perfectly clear-headed and sober tomorrow morning," Annie objected. Her cheeks grew warm, once again.

Maggie stopped at the door to her bedroom and turned. She looked at the pink tinge suffusing Annie's cheeks, threw back her head, and laughed again.

"Oh no, my blushing little virgin friend. I won't give you the chance to ruin your life with second thoughts in the morning." She sounded like the very voice of experience.

She laughed even harder as Annie's face grew scarlet.

Annie sat on the side of her bed, feeling happy and just a little tipsy. She giggled.

The letter is written and mailed, she thought, growing serious. Maggie bullied me into it. At that, I'm glad it's gone and no chance of second thoughts.

I'm so conscious of my body, in a way that I never have been before. This nightie has always made me feel so pretty and feminine. But now I feel naked and vulnerable in it.

She lay down and pulled the covers over herself. Feverishly, she imagined handsome, exuberant Kent beside her. Powerful currents of sensation surged. Her hardened nipples ached.

Apprehension at the thought of sharing a bed with Kent caused her to shiver. What were these odd sensations stirring within her? She felt burningly eager, yet frightened. Would it hurt the first time? Would he be gentle and considerate, or would he be impatient of her inexperience?

As she drifted off into slumber, visions of snow and endless forest populated by wolves and bears swirled through her mind.

She was lost. The wolves' howls were growing closer and she was deathly cold. She needed a fire but the wind kept blowing out her matches.

A furry form burst from the surrounding forest. Terrified, she tried to scream but no sound would come out of her mouth.

She fell, faint, but just before she hit the ground, furry arms interposed. She fell into them. Looking up, she saw that the face inside the fur parka's ruff was Kent's.

He carried her to his cabin, across the sill, and inside. It was lit by the warm flickering light of flames in his fireplace.

There, he lay her on the bear skin, soft and luxurious and joined her. Wonderingly, she noticed that their clothes were gone. When had that happened? How could it have happened without her noticing?

As Kent began to gently explore her nude body, she felt herself responding to his touch, with growing waves of physical sensation that rose and rose to an ultimate crest.

Suddenly, Annie woke, sweat drenched and spent, shaking. Her clock radio was playing. She moaned and waves of heat washed across her face as she recalled the dream.

And, so, three weeks galloped by.

One day, late in August, golden and sunny, they crossed the lobby and walked toward the mail boxes.

"I hope it's there today," Annie said, as they walked. "I'm beginning to fear that we've made fools of ourselves. We have given notice at work and told Mrs. Schmidt...and you've told your dad – and he was rude enough about it. And now, three weeks later, no letter and no tickets. Do you suppose it was all some kind of a sick joke?"

She saw Maggie studying her face and knew that she appeared tired and felt a sad little droop at the corner of her mouth.

Maggie put on her brightest smile and spoke reassuringly, "Don't worry Kid, it'll get here soon. Remember, they said that they only get their mail once a week, so it could really be nearly two weeks before they even got our letters." Having stopped in front of the boxes, she inserted her key.

"You're tired," she said. "And a little hysterical. I can see it in your face. Why don't we leave the rest of the packing until after our last day of work."

Annie shook her head. "It isn't that," she said. "I'm not sleeping well. I get so hyped up that I keep having these dreams, sometimes terribly erotic, but sometimes full of wild animals or freezing or drowning. Or sometimes Kent is mad at me... doesn't like me."

She sighed, and continued, "I'm about to lose my nerve."

As she spoke, she pulled a sheaf of mail from the box. Anxiously, she leafed through it and, suddenly, threw the mail in the air, with a shriek. It cascaded down around her, all over the lobby floor.

She threw her arms around Maggie and danced her around the room. "It's here! It's here!" she squealed.

Then she noticed Mrs. Schmidt standing by the door, staring at them with a startled look. She sobered. Mrs. Schmidt obviously was thinking that her suspicions about their sanity were being confirmed.

Flushing pink, she giggled. "Our tickets came," she explained, stooping to help Maggie gather up the scattered mail.

She giggled again, hugging herself, as they got into the elevator.

"You certainly cheered up in a hurry," Maggie said, with a giggle of her own.

The final week of work sped by and the last day came and went.

They said their good-bys, without regrets.

Now, with only a week remaining, the pace of preparations accelerated, amongst them wild delirious shopping trips for their trousseaus.

In the back of Annie's mind lingered the doubt... a cloud on her happiness. Could she please him? What if she couldn't?

CHAPTER FOUR

"Tomorrow's the day – September fifteenth – North to Alaska!" Maggie proclaimed, as she set the bucket of take-out fried chicken on the table. Behind her, the cupboard gaped emptily. The kitchen sparkled.

"Come on, Annie, quit pacing; sit down, eat. I got chicken so we can just throw everything away when we're done and not make a mess. It's going to be an early morning tomorrow."

"Oh! Maggie. I can't eat. I'm so nervous and excited that I might throw up anyway," Annie replied, "I'm sure to if I eat greasy chicken." She wrung her hands nervously, continuing to pace the floor.

Maggie caught her, put her arms around her, and said, "Annie, come on Kid.You have to eat or you'll be a mess by the time we get to Fairbanks tomorrow evening. Not to mention how you would be by the time you get to our noon wedding at Salchena the next day."

Annie let herself be led to the table and sat. She smiled wistfully and said, "I wish that I could be strong and calm like you, Maggie, but I'm just so happy and frightened and excited and nervous that I could just explode. Or pee my pants anyway. I don't even know if I can go through with this."

Prodded by Maggie, she managed a piece of chicken and a biscuit. Then she excused herself and retired to her room, to check her baggage one last time. Most of their things had been shipped parcel post to Salchena two weeks before.

Annie dressed in her nightie and sank to the bed, there to toss fitfully, seemingly all night. Her head was full of an exhausting whirl. Her dreams went on, and on, and on.

The reddish glow of dawn was just beginning to banish the darkness when Annie groaned and stirred, wakened by Maggie's persistent shaking of her shoulder.

The clock radio, too, had been shipped to Alaska.

Annie groaned again and sat up. Emotionally wrung out, she was exhausted.

"Come on Kid," Maggie coaxed. "Rise and shine. A nice shower will wake you up."

Annie forced an eye open and said, "Ohhh! This is going to be a long day of travel... the plane takes off two hours from now, then four hours to Seattle. Then we have nearly a three hour layover there, followed by three more hours flying to Fairbanks... why, that's almost twelve hours," she said.

Grumbling, she rose and stumbled toward the bathroom. She wore a sleepy, cross expression on her face.

Maggie laughed. "A bride going to her husband is supposed to be joyful," she teased. She followed Annie down the hall and handed her one of the cups of coffee she carried.

Annie stopped, accepted the steaming cup with a grunt of appreciation, and took a large swallow. She felt the potent black brew revitalizing her.

"Ahhh," she said, "That's better." She took another swallow, giggling giddily, as she felt waves of strong emotion surging.

"The butterflies are stomping heavily in my stomach," she said, "but I do feel joyful too... and proud."

At the airport, once they had checked in, Maggie again insisted on Annie joining her for some food.

"But Maggie, I'm just not hungry at all," Annie protested.

"We can't live on love alone," Maggie coaxed. "You have to eat something. We've got two long, strenuous days ahead of us."

She paused, then added teasingly, with a giggle, "Probably

followed by a long and strenuous night." Her face reddened.

Annie giggled, too, a little hysterically, her cheeks glowing rosily. She said, "Hush, Maggie, or I won't be able to get on the plane."

Resigned, she allowed herself to be led to the restaurant. There she sat and picked at the scrambled eggs and toast, until the last bite had finally been forced down.

She gulped the last swallow of her milk and got up, saying nervously, "Let's go, Maggie. It's only fifteen minutes until boarding time."

The next half hour was a hectic one. At the end of it, the two friends were seated side by side on a jumbo jet as it taxied into take off position.

Annie looked rigidly out the window, watching the activity. Her face was pale and she saw that her knuckles were white, when she glanced down to where her hands gripped the seat arms tightly.

She stared out the window, then tore her gaze away from the asphalt speeding by and looked at her friend. "Maggie, I've never flown before, either," she confessed, nervously.

"Relax Annie," Maggie said and laughed. "It's perfectly safe. There are going to be lots of things happening to you for the first time this next few days. Relax and enjoy it." She waggled her eyebrows, leered, and laughed again.

Responding with a laugh, Annie found that she was, indeed, relaxing.

Maggie kept to herself the fact that this was her first experience flying, and that she was a little nervous too – just as she had concealed, behind a bold front, the fact that her experience of sex was limited and she, too, was anticipating her wedding night with not a little nervousness.

The plane roared down the runway and lifted into the air making the city swiftly vanish beneath them, as they rose above the clouds.

Golden sun shone upon the great puffy billows of white clouds. The sky was bright and blue. It was an omen, she felt. The odd feeling in her stomach settled down. Her spirits lifted.

With a contemplative expression, she turned to Annie. "This is the end of one phase of our existence and the start of a new one," she said.

An hour passed. The stewardess brought a lunch that looked and smelled good. But Annie rebelled at Maggie's attempt to coerce her into eating again.

She was content to watch, as Maggie enjoyed the meal. Eventually, the trays were collected and more time passed, seeming to drag by. Then she heard the pitch of the engines change and felt the plane begin to descend. With a crackle and hum, the public address system came to life and the pilot announced their imminent landing in Seattle.

The touchdown was so gentle that she never did identify the exact moment of landing.

Annie gazed out the restaurant window at the runway, busy with jets coming and going. With a glance at her watch, she said, "Finally! We have less than an hour to wait for our flight to Alaska."

Maggie looked sourly at her third cup of coffee. Then she laughed and said, "Thank God. If I drank one more cup of this awful coffee, I would float away. Let's go freshen up and walk on down to our gate."

Unhurried, they strolled to the ladies room, stopping to buy fresh magazines at a news stand, along the way.

Glancing at Maggie, who was running a comb through her red curls, she said, "You look terrific. That deep sky blue skirt and jacket match your eyes and complement your red hair marvelously. And the pastel blue blouse, purse and shoes are perfect."

Annie studied herself in the mirror and added, "I'm worried about my outfit, though. I liked it, before, but now I don't know. Is it too vivid?" She frowned nervously at her image, trying to see it through Kent's eyes.

Annie's emerald green, full-skirted dress brought out the honey tone in her brown hair and made her changeable eyes take on a glowing green tone.

It was an expensive dress, bought for her wedding trip, and the elegant tailoring of the bodice clung to her upper body, emphasizing the swell of her bosom and hips, the slenderness of her waist. Shoes and purse matched the dress.

Maggie looked at her admiringly. "Don't worry, Kid. You'll knock his eyes out," she reassured. Then, with a glance down at her watch, she exclaimed, "Only half an hour 'til boarding. We better hustle."

Three hours travel north, found Annie staring out the window at the rugged mountainous folds in the earth. Mile after mile of them, rising bare and rocky to caps of snow and ice. She shivered – and glanced, yet again, at her watch.

Maggie noticed and said, "It does look cold and desolate. There has been no sign of human presence for over an hour." She paused, then added, with a smile, "Haven't your eyes worn the face off that watch yet?"

With a real effort, Annie forced a smile and said, "Only half an hour more to Fairbanks. I'm so full of adrenalin that I can hardly stand it... so nervous that I feel almost faint."

Maggie squeezed her hand sympathetically. "Hang in there, Kid, the worst of it will be over in half an hour. Then we will be there and have met them."

With another weak smile, Annie replied, "I'm thankful that we are doing this together. It isn't so bad as doing something like this all by myself. I'm not sure that I could."

The plane left the mountains behind and began to descend across a vast swampy meadow that stretched as far as she could see, disappearing into the distance. All was green... a green wilderness, still, with no sign of life.

The cabin speaker crackled to life, "Passengers will now please place their seats and tray tables in an upright position. We will be landing at Fairbanks in approximately fifteen minutes."

The swamp continued to flow beneath them, mile after mile, seemingly endless. Annie gulped, trying to swallow, but her mouth was suddenly dry. The nervousness swelled and roiled in her stomach, causing her to moan, "Oh, I feel almost sick."

Maggie was silent and a furtive glance revealed a curious, set, expression on her face. And her eyes... did they look curiously moist? Annie wondered.

While the plane settled lower and lower, she gazed out the window and down. The swampy ground was very close. Had the pilot made a mistake? Surely they weren't going to land in this swamp.

She clutched the seat arms tightly, swallowing convulsively as she glanced again at her friend. Maggie still wore that odd, set expression.

As she turned her attention back to the view out the window, the plane swept, suddenly, across the rolling waters of a wide grey river. A low range of hills burst into view ahead of them and solid ground just below them.

Then the plane landed with a gentle bounce and rolled down the runway toward a low-lying terminal building. There must be a city around... somewhere in this wilderness.

But there was a man waiting for her here, a stranger.

Panic rose in her throat and she felt the sting of threatened tears in her eyes. Annie jerked, startled, as Maggie reassuringly clutched her arm, saying, "Hang in there, Kid, we've almost got it made."

Maggie looked pale and serious, her freckles standing out against an unusually pale complexion. Almost as though she suffered from the same doubts... but that was a ridiculous thought. Maggie was a tough one, after all.

The plane eased to a stop and the accordion-walled loading ramp eased up against the door with a gentle thump. Then followed a wait that seemed interminable, before the doors were opened.

Passengers surged by her, down the aisle and off the plane. The initial surge gone by, Annie got up, dazedly. The plane was nearly empty... what would Kent and Blaine think, that they hadn't come? She turned to a strangely pale and frozen Maggie and grasped her hand, pulling her to her feet.

With a ghastly little smile, Maggie said, "Here goes, Kid. It's been nice knowing you."

Annie heard herself giggling hysterically.

They began to move down the aisle, following out the last stragglers of the other passengers. All the colors seemed unusually bright and it seemed that everything was moving in slow motion. Annie floated down the aisle and into the ramp.

What ever had possessed her to do this? How could she have been so foolish? Oh, what if Kent wasn't there? Or, worse, maybe she wouldn't recognize him.

Hysteria started to rise in her as she visualized him saying that he had changed his mind, rejecting her. Then, suddenly, she burst from the ramp. Desperately, she looked around the room, looking for him.

An agonizingly beautiful, rugged, bronzed giant floated across the room toward her, moving in slow motion, it seemed.

Oh, she hadn't realized that he was so tall, she thought distractedly, or so broad shouldered.

He enfolded her in his arms. While she gazed up at him, it seemed that his face drifted down toward hers. Her lips parted instinctively and he took them firmly with his.

Her blood and her consciousness flowed to her lips and she surrendered unconditionally. Seemingly of their own accord, her arms crept up around his neck and all thought disappeared in a whirl of sensation.

Smelling her hair appreciatively, he caressed her cheek with his. His lips trailed down the left side of her neck and rose again to her ear, to whisper, "Welcome to your new home in Alaska. You are even more beautiful than your pictures."

She clung to him convulsively, until he kissed her gently on the cheek and said, "Introduce me to your friend."

Annie unwound herself from Kent, flushing as she realized how she had molded herself against him. She turned to find Maggie.

She was melted against a tall man, who seemed to be trying to devour her. As she watched, Maggie was finally released and turned to them.

Maggie's face was heatedly flushed and her eyes had a spent, dreaming look. Her lips appeared swollen and extraordinarily red. In her vivid blue eyes, glowed a great dawning light. Annie had never seen her look more beautiful.

The two couples exchanged introductions, all the while eyeing each other shyly.

"Let's go get your bags," Kent exclaimed. "Then we can get you checked into your rooms, before we take you out to dinner."

Annie grasped his arm, blindly letting him lead her along as she gazed up at him, hanging on his every word.

They paused, waiting for the line into the baggage claim area to clear. Her attention all focused on Kent, it was with a shock that she, suddenly, became aware of a great furry form towering over her, as had happened in her dreams.

"Ohhh!" she squeaked, the scream half muffled in the constriction of her throat. She sprang back, colliding with Kent.

With a hearty laugh, he put his arms around her, saying, "It's dead – and stuffed. He's a fine specimen of an Alaskan grizzly bear."

Breathless sounding, Maggie said, "Oh, he's a huge monster." She stared up at the towering height of him. It was mounted standing erect on its hind legs, its front paws spread wide and mouth open in a snarl. His teeth were huge.

Blaine grinned and replied, "He isn't an exceptionally big one, as bears go, only nine feet tall. He always impresses the Cheechakos though."

"Cheechakos?" Maggie asked, one eyebrow shot up quizzically. Sometimes she was annoyed with herself, but she could not control her expressive face.

Blaine noted the expression with an affectionate smile. "Newcomers to the Arctic," he explained. "It means about the same thing as Tenderfoot."

Annie glanced apprehensively at the bear once again as the line moved on into the claim area. Those claws looked six inches long and razor sharp, too. She certainly wanted nothing to do with one of those.

In a short while, the couples had collected the baggage and emerged from the airport, shivering in the cool September air. Kent and Blaine led them to a waiting limousine.

The uniformed chauffeur helped the breathless young ladies into a plush interior, two velvet sofas facing each other in the rear of the vehicle. He turned to the task of loading the luggage into the trunk.

Kent and Blaine slid into the limousine and Kent extracted a bottle of champagne from an ice bucket. He opened it, extracting the cork with a pop, and began to fill four lovely long-stemmed champagne glasses.

Taking the glass that he offered, Annie sipped appreciatively. He paused and she gazed into his eyes over the rim of the glass. She should pinch herself but she hoped that, if this was a dream, it would never end.

His gaze was direct, penetrating, a challenge to meet.

Softly, she said, "This limousine is a real surprise. Certainly, it's the last thing we would've expected here on the Arctic frontier."

Kent grinned proudly, continuing to fill the glasses and hand them around. "We rented it for today and tomorrow," he responded.

Taking the last glass for himself, he raised it and said, "Here's a toast... To a long and happy marriage for all of us."

Between sips of champagne, Annie giggled. "I have to confess that I was so nervous I could hardly get off the plane," she explained, "but now I feel positively giddy with relief." With another giggle, she sipped again at her glass, which Kent had refilled.

Kent laughed heartily. "Blaine and I were a bit shaky in the knees ourselves... Weren't we, Pardner?" he said, glancing across to where Blaine was tenderly holding Maggie's hand and gazing soulfully into her eyes.

Blaine looked at Annie, a slow sleepy looking smile on his face. "You bet we were," he drawled. "But it's all better now."

Fairbanks seemed tiny... a village. Nothing seemed to be more than three or four stories tall.

The limousine pulled up before the Regency Hotel and the driver

turned off the engine.

"Well, here we are,"Blaine said."I think that this is Fairbanks' best."

The chauffeur sprang out and opened the door, offering his hand to the ladies in turn, to assist them out of the vehicle.

As they walked into the lobby, Kent said, "We got you rooms with Jacuzzi baths. We thought that perhaps you would like an hour or so to enjoy them and rest, before dinner."

He glanced at his watch. "It's five o'clock now, Fairbanks time," he said. "Shall we meet here in the lobby at six-thirty?"

Annie nodded.

They arrived at the desk. As their men checked them in, she looked at her watch. Eight o'clock, it read. It had, indeed, been a long day since Maggie had gotten her up at six that morning.

She grasped the stem and reset her watch to local time.

The bell boy led them to their adjoining rooms and deposited their luggage there.

Annie wasted no time starting the huge jacuzzi tub filling with steaming water. A dozen red roses and a bottle of champagne, prominently displayed on a table beside the tub, brought a tender smile to her face.

"He is so thoughtful," she exclaimed.

She kicked off her shoes and gladly peeled off her clothes. With relief, she relaxed in her slip, sipping at a glass of champagne she had poured herself.

The tub filled. Annie poured herself another glass of champagne and eased herself into the steaming water, sighing with satisfaction, and sipped the champagne. The roses were beautiful.

Tenderly she touched her lips, running a forefinger along them. No man had ever stirred such a response, indeed she had never even imagined herself experiencing feelings such as Kent had evoked. A not unpleasant tension stirred within her body.

Then, for a moment, her mood was spoiled. Her mother's face floated before her mind's eye. Mother always said that nice girls don't do that. Nice girls don't feel the way I am feeling.

Annie froze up a little, guilt warring with the pounding of her pulse and the flow of her natural juices.

"Sorry Mom. I guess that I'm not going to be a nice girl, by your standards. But, Mom, I'm going to be happy... surely that should count for something?" she pleaded.

It seemed that she could see Mom smile and nod. The feelings of guilt diminished. Of course, Mom hadn't meant that for a married woman... had she? Reflecting on Dad and Mom, the way they were together... so happy, she knew Mom hadn't meant that for a married woman.

She snapped out of her reverie with a start. A hasty glance at her watch, lying there on the table, revealed that nearly an hour had slipped away while she dreamed.

What should she wear? The gold sheath with its matching stiletto-heeled shoes, she decided, flushing guiltily at the memory of the shopping spree she and Maggie had gone on.

Uncomfortably, she was aware that she was coming nearly penniless to her husband. But, then, buying a trousseau is a once in a life time event, she rationalized, as she briskly toweled herself dry.

She unpacked her dress for this evening and hung her wedding dress in the closet. A lovely filmy white dress, knee length and full skirted, it had matching white heels. She would wear the string of pearls inherited from her mother.

The string of pearls was something old, she thought with a smile. Blue garters, borrowed from Maggie, handled the something borrowed and something blue, all in one fell swoop.

I wish Mom could be there tomorrow, she thought, wistfully. There were times since her Mom's death that she had missed her terribly.

She shook herself, determinedly rejecting sadness. Look at the time, it was already nearly six-thirty.

There was a soft rapping on the door as she hastily finished dressing.

"Are you ready?" called Maggie.

Annie hurried across the room and opened the door. She said, "I'm ready, I think. Do I look ok?"

Maggie scanned her and gave a low whistle. "Very nice," she replied, "But we had better hurry."

Maggie's dress was black and slinky. Blaine would be struck dumb, Annie thought.

As they entered the lobby, they found Kent and Blaine deep in conversation. Kent glanced up, noticed them, and came swiftly across the room to welcome Annie with a gentle kiss. Blaine was only moments behind.

A table waited for them in the dining room and they were no sooner seated than a waiter appeared with hors d'oeuvres.

Smiling, Kent explained, "We took the liberty of ordering for you...Blaine and I have something else to start this meal off right."

He looked at Blaine and nodded.

Blaine grinned and continued the conversation, "And a one, and a two, and a three... ta da!" Together the men each opened a small box and held it out for inspection.

"Blaine! It's beautiful," gasped Maggie, gazing at the large solitaire diamond, set on a golden nugget band.

Blaine slipped the ring onto her finger and continued to hold her hand. "The nugget band is traditional for Alaskans... our history is so interwoven with gold and mining," he said.

"What's the matter Annie?... Don't you like it?" Kent's distressed voice caught their attention.

Annie was staring at a large ruby, surrounded by small emeralds, also on a golden nugget band. Tears streamed down her face and she nibbled at her lower lip.

She sobbed and answered with obvious difficulty, "Oh, yes. It's the most lovely thing I've ever seen." She sobbed again. "I'm just crying because I'm so happy," she choked out. Then, with a weak smile, she said, "Dumb, huh?"

A smile lit Kent's features. "No, not dumb. I'm glad you like it."

He grasped her hand and slipped the ring on her finger, following it with a kiss. Taking a handkerchief from his pocket, he gently dried her tears and dabbed at the smeared make-up beneath her eyes. "I've always preferred the colored stones," he said.

Maggie looked smilingly at Annie's smudged face. "It has been a long, emotional day," Maggie excused her. She bravely suppressed a sympathetic sting in her eyes and added, "Let me take her to the ladies room."

"Of course," said Kent. Blaine added his nod. She rose and led Annie off, conscious of Blaine's eyes stroking her calves.

Returning refreshed, Maggie and Annie picked distractedly at their food, hardly noticing the excellence of the meal. The long day had been too overwhelming.They hung on the conversation of their men.

Kent and Blaine kept the conversation light, telling humorous anecdotes of their country with an infectious enthusiasm for their topic.

At length, Blaine asked, "Would you like dessert? Or maybe an after dinner drink?"

"Thank you, but no," Maggie replied. With a glance at her watch, she said, "It's nearly eleven by my watch, I haven't changed it yet. So it's time that we should probably both get to bed, so that we can be fresh and rested for our wedding."

Annie nodded and rose with a smile, saying, "Thank you for the ring, and for dinner."

Blaine and Kent, she saw, were starting to rise. She stopped them with a raised hand. "No," she said, "you two enjoy an after dinner drink. We will see you in the morning."

Going to Kent, she bestowed a soft kiss on him.

Kent held her hand a moment. "We have to get flowers and attend to some details in the morning. You girls may as well get breakfast and be ready to leave by ten-thirty. We'll come to your rooms then."

Snuggled into her bed, Annie tossed and turned, a whirl of thoughts in her head. He seemed a nice man, and considerate. She was already half in love with him. Would he love her too? Oh, what a tragedy, if he did not come to do so.

She hoped he would be gentle. When she had her checkup and blood tests, the doctor had cautioned her that there may be some pain the first time but then it would get better. Fervently, she wished that she wasn't such a sissy about pain.

That bear in the airport was huge and frightening. What an awful thing to put there. Surely there weren't many of them around here. Oh! She was too over-tired and she would never go to sleep, she thought, wildly.

CHAPTER FIVE

Annie jerked upright in bed, her heart pounding. What was that awful noise? The penetrating shriek of the telephone continued to nag her. What a nauseating tone! Guaranteed not only to wake the dead, but to also raise their blood pressure at least ten points.

She had gone to sleep just moments ago. What could this call be? She swung her legs to the floor and groped for the annoying instrument, her eyes seeming glued shut.

The telephone continued to shriek. Desperately, she felt around atop the bed stand.

With a bang, she succeeded in knocking the telephone to the floor. Finally, she located the receiver and raised it to her ear, to hear, "Good morning, this is the seven a.m.wake up call you requested." The operator spoke in a revoltingly nice voice.

"Uhnh," Annie grunted crossly, "Ok." She stretched her shoulders. "Please send me a pot of coffee and a hot buttered cheese Danish."

"Certainly, Miss," the phone replied cheerily. It clicked.

Annie hung up the receiver with an emphatic bang, then winced. How could people be so despicably cheerful at this hour? Oh... it didn't feel like she had slept at all, but she had to get ready for her hair appointment at eight thirty.

She wandered into the bathroom. "I know how to get going,"she muttered, as she climbed into the shower. She turned the water on all the way to the cold setting, then, bracing herself, she pulled the shower knob.

"Ooohh!" she muffled a shriek, then scrubbed her face and eyes deliberately in the icy blast. Moderating the temperature, she finished washing herself. She did not linger, but dried herself and donned her robe, to be ready for room service, which arrived shortly thereafter.

Two cups of coffee and a Danish completed her revival and she began to feel excited and cheerful.

The rest of the day was a mad whirl for Annie and Maggie. First there was the hair dresser. Then helping each other into their gowns was more time-consuming a process than they had thought and barely complete, when their grooms arrived with the limousine to whisk them off to the Salchena Lodge for the joint wedding.

During the ride to the lodge, there was more champagne. The mood was merry.

To her eyes, the countryside was fascinating, a welcome relief from the city. The road side seemed a sea of golden leaves, broken, here and there, by green spruce and crimson splashes of cranberry and currant brush.The land appeared to be deliciously uninhabited. It rolled, forest covered, to a snow capped range of hills on her left. Ahead, towered the rugged, rocky peaks of the Alaska Range.

Kent sipped at his champagne and explained, "The Salchena Lodge is a roadhouse on the highway. It has a big restaurant, some rooms, and gas pumps. Aside from serving the highway traffic, though, it's a social center for those of us who live in the forests of the Salchena River valley. All of our friends will be there for the wedding."

And, indeed, the lodge was swarming with people who looked, somehow, as though they belonged in the forest. Their gaze was more direct and their manner of speech more straightforward than the girls were accustomed to. Clean jeans and plaid wool shirts passed for formal wear for most. Many of the men were bearded.

Again, Annie found herself beset by doubts..."Oh, my God, what the Hell am I doing? I don't even know this man." Across the room, she saw Maggie laughing gaily at something a strange woman had said. Half hysterically, she wondered, "How can she laugh? We are about to make a terrible mistake and she doesn't even realize it."

Maggie and Annie were not allowed long for nerves to set in, for soon the strains of the wedding march filled the air.

The minister stood at the front of the room. Merrily he cried, "Let the brides and grooms come before me."

In a daze, Annie let Kent lead her forward. Blaine, she noticed, had led a subdued-looking Maggie forward also. Both the men wore new looking black suits.

She responded when prompted by the minister. It was like she was in a dream that culminated in Kent taking her in his arms for a kiss. The dream had a familiar quality. It should, she thought, for she had been dreaming it for weeks.With hot, flushed cheeks, she remembered what happened next, in her dreams.Now she knew why brides blush.

The two new brides were overwhelmed by the massive offering of simple friendship.At the party following the wedding, dance followed dance endlessly. Every man in Alaska, it seemed, wanted to dance with the new brides, and every wife wanted to offer them advice.

There was punch, delicious punch to a thirsty Annie... she later learned it was made of Hawaiian Punch, orange juice and orange sherbet, with dry ice floated in it, and fifty percent vodka.The side tables also held cakes and little sandwiches. The punch was smooth going down, especially after the fifth or sixth cup, but Annie found that, unexplainably, it made her giddy.

"Whoo-eee, Kent," she heard a lanky woodsman bellow (he had been drinking quite a lot of the punch, too, she had noticed), "Suits and ties...You and Blaine are so duded up, we reckoned you must be Seattle peddlers, at first look – come up north to rip off us yokels."

The north country, she was to find, nourished a profound distrust of men who wear suits and ties.

Six o'clock found Annie near exhaustion, her feet and legs aching from the unaccustomed high-heeled shoes. She considered kicking them off, and dancing barefoot. No, it wouldn't be lady-like, she decided. She settled for another cup of punch – and felt slightly better.

About that time, genuine relief washed through her to hear Kent say, to a friend, "Sorry, men, but we have to get changed and be away, so that we can reach the homestead before dark. It's coming on that time of year when it gets pretty black out in those woods."

He put his arm around her and led her off to one of the rooms.

Maggie had been rescued and escorted there by Blaine, only a few minutes earlier.

"Why it's Mrs. Winfield, I do believe," Maggie said, with a laugh. She took blue jeans from a suitcase and pulled them on.

"Oh yes, Mrs. Burns," Annie said, dreamily. "Oh Maggie, can you believe it? I've been just floating through this whole day like it was a dream." She giggled, uncontrollably, hearing the rising pitch of her own voice, then covered her mouth guiltily.

Maggie tossed her head, her red curls bouncing, as she responded, "I know. The wedding itself and meeting all Kent's and Blaine's friends. After the trip yesterday, it's all overwhelming."

After Maggie studied Annie's flushed face, she accused, "And you have been into the punch bowl, once too often. That giggle was a dead give away."

Annie giggled again, and said, "Only a little. Don't worry, it'll wear off on the ride home."

She pulled on her own jeans and reached for one of her new plaid flannel shirts. Earnestly, she confided, "And now we are changing for the trip to our new homes in the Bush. I'm happy but it's all so much, so fast, that I feel all wound up."

Maggie stopped buttoning her shirt and laid her hand on her friend's shoulder. She gazed earnestly into her eyes. "It will be all right, Annie," she said, reassuringly. "Now you'll have three weeks of peace to get settled in, then we'll all go to town shopping and see the place. Won't that be fun?"

Annie smiled mistily, replying, "Yes it will. But... Maggie?"At her friend's glance, she continued, "I'm still nervous about tonight, about well... you know... sex."

There was a moment of silence, each of the girls thinking her own thoughts.

Then Annie grinned, wryly, adding, "Nervous, *hell*, I'm *terrified*!" She felt her face growing rosy.

"Aw, Kid," Maggie said compassionately, "it'll be fine. Every woman in the world, since the beginning of time, has survived this, you know."

Maggie finished buttoning her shirt and pulled on her boots. She said hesitantly, "If it helps you to know this, I'm a little scared myself. I guess it's natural to wonder how it will be. And to fear that he won't be pleased."

She studied Annie, then confessed, "I have already fallen head over heels for Blaine and I desperately want to please him."

Annie pulled on her new boots, and stood. She brightened and replied, "It does help. I don't feel so alone, when I know that you're scared too."

A knocking came at the door. "Are you ready, girls?" It was Kent's voice. "We have to get going so that we can make it home before dark."

"Coming," Annie called. She caught Maggie in a quick, fierce hug. "Good luck," she whispered, then stepped to the door and opened it.

Kent caught her in his strong arms and brushed his lips across hers, leaving an exciting tingling.

"You must be exhausted," he said, with a laugh. His brown eyes danced with laughter, smile wrinkles at their corners.

She joined him in his laugh. "I am indeed," she exclaimed. "I must have danced with every man in the state of Alaska."

"Surely not more than half," he retorted. He picked up her case, into which she had stuffed her wedding gown. To Maggie, he said, "Well, Mrs. Burns, Blaine will be along for you in a few minutes. Annie and I must start on our way."

She followed him down the hall and out to his pickup truck. While they were changing clothes, it seemed, most of the revelers had disappeared, headed for their homes in the forests. "Where did they all come from?" she asked, "I wouldn't have thought anyone lived here, much less all these people."

He laughed. "Well, darling, you have to remember that this is a big, big country. The Salchena valley, alone, is over ten thousand square miles. Now you figure maybe one person for every fifty square miles and you get... about two hundred people live here."

Robin, the motherly postmistress and owner of the lodge, stopped her for a hug. "You have a good man, Annie," she said, "take good care of him."

Annie blushed, and nodded. Robin, she saw, had gone all out for the wedding and wore a full skirted, lavender, satin dress.

Nestled against Kent, as he drove out onto the highway, Annie held out her left hand admiring her rings. For the ceremony today, Kent had placed a second ring on her finger, a wide plain gold nuggeted band. The two rings were a beautiful set and their symbolism was important to her.

"Mrs. Kent Winfield! she whispered, trying out the sound of her new name once again, "Annie Winfield."

Kent tightened his arm around her shoulders and gave her a squeeze. "Sound good?" he asked, softly.

"Mmhm," she said and nodded.

The drive on the highway lasted only a few minutes. Then the truck slowed and Kent turned on the signal.

Withdrawing his arm, he said, "Sorry, but I have to use both hands from here on."

She snuggled closer against him.

Unbelieving, she saw where they were headed and tensed, expecting a sudden collision. She stared out the windshield, as he drove the truck off the highway and between two large spruce trees. They made it through the narrow gap between the trees, and bounced over a mound. Then she noticed that they were on a narrow, dirt road – really just a pair of wheel tracks leading off, through the forest.

Annie rolled down the window, sniffing appreciatively at the autumn scented air. It was mild, with just a hint of the coming evening chill.

"This is just gorgeous," she breathed. Clumps of birch and cottonwood trees glowed in their suits of golden leaves. The willows, and the lower brush, too, glowed golden,yellow and brown.

Here and there, high bush cranberry and currant brush again lent a vivid splash of color with their crimson leaves. Scattered through it all were the green spruce.

A rabbit hopped unconcernedly out of the road and, a ways further, several large black birds exploded into flight, their wings thundering in the still air.

"What are those," Annie gasped, startled.

"Spruce grouse," Ken replied, "Good eating."

The road narrowed more. In places, branches scraped the truck as they went by. There had been no sign of habitation since they left the highway.

"Oh!" she exclaimed, "Look at the big dog. Who does he belong to?"

The grey animal faded furtively into the brush.

Kent laughed heartily and replied, "That, my Cheechako sweetheart, is no dog – it's a wolf."

Annie shivered. The wolf brought home to her the fact that this was a true wilderness, quite unlike the settled and developed farm country she had grown up in.

Somehow, she had not realized the real meaning of the word "wilderness." She shivered again. Now, she was beginning to understand.

With a wry attempt at humor, she muttered, under her breath, "Something tells me that we aren't in Kansas anymore, Toto." The wizard of Oz had been one of her favorite childhood movies. This was not a yellow brick road, but there was an equal sense of unreality.

They drove on and, lulled by the motion of the truck, she dozed off, her head nestling on his strong shoulder. Wakened by some instinct, she jerked erect, looked out the front windshield, and saw that the truck was headed directly for a creek, much too fast to stop in time.

"Kent!" she squealed.

Her pulse pounded in her temples and she felt a surge of adrenalin. She slid forward to the edge of the seat, bracing herself against the dashboard and floor boards.

The truck bounced and lurched, then threw up a sheet of spray as it splashed across the shallow creek and lurched into a packed earth clearing before a rustic cabin.

She gasped in relief and sank back limp and breathless.

Kent chuckled. "Sorry, I should've warned you about the creek but I thought that you were asleep," he apologized. "This is Blaine's place."

The cabin looked considerably more rough hewn than she remembered from the pictures. More rustic and less romantic.

With dismay, she hoped that Kent's looked better.

Then, casually, he informed her, "This is the end of the good road."

Annie glanced at him to see if he was joking. "Good road?"she asked, weakly.

"We go on by three wheeler from here," he explained, indicating an oversized tricycle with massive balloon tires.

She gazed about her, noting bald rocky peaks rising ahead of them, already snow capped. The rocky lower portions appeared blue, with distance. A narrow path wound into the brush before the three wheeler.

Kent had already gotten out of the truck and was busy strapping her luggage onto the machine. Feeling foolish and dependent, she slid from the truck and went to stand beside him, watching, helplessly. She wanted to do something, but had not the faintest idea of what to do.

"Your other things came a few days ago, and I've already hauled them home," he said. He reached down and started the machine.

Settling onto the front of the seat, he patted the seat cushion behind him. He said, "You sit here behind me. We control the direction of travel partly with body weight, by leaning left to help steer left and so on. Don't worry, it's easy. You'll get the hang of it right away."

She still stood there.

"Hop on," he ordered. Peremptorily, she thought.

With dismay, she edged toward the machine.

Gingerly, she climbed on and straddled the seat behind him.

He had told her about this in his letters but, obviously, her imagination had not been equal to the task of understanding the things he was telling her. There were a lot of things, it appeared, that she had failed to imagine properly.

Numbly, she wondered what other shocks lay in store for her.

"It gets bumpy. Hold on tight, with both hands around my waist and you'll be fine," he reassured her.

Annie was not reassured. Apprehensively, she hugged him tightly about the waist. As she did, her eyes fell upon a large black pistol, hanging in a sheath from the handle bars.

"What's the gun for?"she stammered, blanching. She had learned the city dwellers irrational fear of guns.

"Oh, that. It's just in case we meet an unfriendly bear or wolf," he drawled, nonchalantly, "Unlikely, but I prefer to be prepared.You need to be able to handle the guns, too. They're an important tool and means of defense, up here. I'll teach you to shoot later this week."

She absorbed that silently, filing it away for later thought. On the farm, she had, of course, used a twenty-two rifle for rabbits and grouse. But nothing else. That pistol looked big enough to tear her arm off with its recoil.

"I thought that wolves wouldn't attack people?" she objected.

"Healthy ones generally don't, though you never know – depends on how hungry they are," he replied. "Unfortunately, there's a persistent problem with a number of them carrying hydrophobia." — "Rabies," he explained, sensing her puzzlement, "It causes them to attack without fear or restraint."

He glanced back over his shoulder, again. "Ready?" he asked.

Numb with fear, she nodded her head, wordlessly. The noise of the engine grew louder and the machine jumped forward, with a lurch, bounced over several bumps, and smacked down a bush as it entered the trail.The bush hit the ground with a whack, and she giggled, though nothing was funny.

"Just what," she wondered, "have I gotten myself into?" Her mutter was lost in the engine noise.

Every muscle in her body was clenched as they started on toward Kent's cabin. But five minutes accustomed her to the swaying rhythm of the ride. The trail seemed to widen slightly, once they entered the forest.

She relaxed slightly and asked, "How much longer is it?"

"Only about half an hour," he yelled over the engine noise.

It was beginning to get dusky. She felt chilled – and big, fluffy snow flakes began to drift from the darkening sky.

Reflected light from the headlight shone from the trees and brush. Beyond the tunnel of light, the forest had a foreboding atmosphere of gloom, haunted, the abode of creatures of the dark.

Soon, a light covering of snow blanketed the ground. It continued to drift from the sky, filling the headlight beam with flurries of white.

Through a break in the clouds, a fringe of fiery, orange sky outlined the ragged peaks ahead.

"Creek coming up," Kent called over his shoulder. "Rocky and bumpy. Hang on tight. If one side bounces up, lean that direction."

She saw the gleam of water in the headlights, it was wide, but apparently shallow, if he was going to try to drive across it. She hoped he wasn't making a mistake.

Water splashed up as they hit the edge of the creek. At that moment, she spotted a large, black, hairy animal across the creek and just down stream. It stood there, just in the edge of the headlights beam, threatening eyes gleaming with reflected light.

Her heart thundered in her chest, as she recalled the huge animal on display in the airport.

"It's a bear!"she screamed in Kent's ear. "A grizzly bear!" Just then the right rear wheel hit a rock and the down stream side of the machine began to rise.

Panic stricken, her only thought to escape the bear and to avoid being crushed by the falling machine, she let go of Kent and struggled to get off the upstream side of the three wheeler.

Her despairing shriek rang in the air as she lost her balance, clutched at Kent, and fell anyway. It seemed that she was suspended in the air, falling, forever. She was going to be killed on her wedding night... drowned and eaten.

There was a double splash. In shock, she felt the ice cold water close over her head. This water was deep, he had driven her right into water that was over her head. And she couldn't swim. Struggling, she regretted not have taken swimming lessons, when the Red Cross had offered them.

As she floundered in the water, her lungs near bursting, she felt Kent grasp her and draw her to her feet. She gasped for air, feeling it burn into her lungs, cold and fresh. The water lapped around her knees, cold as ice.

Kent hugged her. He tried to give her a kiss, but she shook him off angrily. They still were in danger.

"Now is no time for kissing!" she snapped. "Where's the bear?"

Kent began to laugh. He laughed until tears ran from his eyes, pointing to the far bank, with an arm that dripped water all along its length.

Annie was enraged. Never the less, her eyes followed his pointing finger to where the three-wheeler sat, purring quietly on the bank.

Evidently, once it was relieved of their weight, it had settled back down and run on out of the creek. The animal stood sniffing at it curiously.

"It's just a small cow moose," Kent gasped out, as he got his laughter under control. Water dripped from his hat and ran down his face.

He saw her shiver and noticed the angry glare she had turned on him. Sobered, he said, "I'm sorry, sweetheart, it's only one more mile. I'll get you there and build a fire for you to warm up at."

As an after thought, he added, "This is the reason they quit making three-wheelers – went to four-wheelers, instead, because they're more stable."

"I don't feel much like a sweetheart now," she protested, "How could you laugh at me?" Her already protruding lip began to tremble, as she fought back the threat of scalding tears.

The moose had moved away, she saw, as she suppressed the tears with an effort and let him lead her to the machine and help her on.

The fact that he had laughed at her stung. That had been a really frightening experience... and he *laughed*. Wistfully, she longed for him to be more sensitive.

By now it was dark. Fearsome shapes lurked dimly at the edges of the headlight beam as they went. It seemed that hours passed before they stopped in front of a cabin.

In the night, it loomed dark and cavernous, forbidding. She clung to Kent more tightly, frightened and numb with cold. Her fingers had lost feeling, she discovered.

He left the engine running and light on. Gently, he disengaged himself from her grip. "Wait here," he said. "I'll start the electric generator so that we have some lights."

"No!" she exclaimed, grabbing his hand and clinging to it, "... I'm coming with you." Her heart hammered with fright, as she slid off the machine. Her feet were half asleep. They prickled with pain, as she put her weight on them.

He led her by the hand to a small building, across the clearing, that was picked out by the headlight. There he pressed a button and an engine sprang to life.

Suddenly, the yard was lit by a bright floodlight and soft, lamp light streamed from the front room window. She felt herself begin to relax marginally. Dismayed, she saw that Kent's cabin looked every bit as rustic as Blaine's had but maybe it would look better in the day light, tomorrow.

"What are those heavy grates covering the windows," she asked, "like a jail?"

"They are to make it harder for bears to break in," Kent replied.

"What a reassuring thought. It does wonders for my state of mind." she muttered, inaudibly.

Drawn to the friendly, yellow light, she walked into the cabin. It was bright, at least, but a large thermometer on the wall read twenty-five degrees. No wonder she was numb – half frozen, in her wet clothes.

The sound of the three-wheeler ceased and Kent entered with her two suitcases. Setting them down, he crossed to a large iron stove and threw in kindling, a scoop of sawdust soaked in kerosene and some large chunks of split spruce.

At the touch of a match, a cheerful, orange blaze roared to life. He forced her into a rocking chair, drawn close to the open stove door. The fire felt good, very good.

"Sit here," he ordered her; "I'll have hot water going in the shower within fifteen minutes." She watched him resentfully, as he walked into a different room. What made him think he could give her orders?

Annie examined her surroundings. The room very obviously belonged to a man. It was stark, no curtains at the windows, no decorations or touches of color. No flounces or pillows or anything to soften the hard lines of the room.

The wall hangings were exclusively practical – guns, traps, snowshoes, a cast iron skillet, fly fishing rods and so on.

A mild sense of depression settled upon her spirit.

She tugged off her clammy boots and socks. Gratefully, she held her aching feet near the fire. The returning circulation stung sharply.

Annie's wet clothes began to steam in the heat radiating from the stove. Her face and ears felt flushed, hot, as the blood rushed back to the surface of her skin. Sharp, biting pain in her fingers heralded their return to life, bringing brief tears to her eyes which she dashed away angrily.

Her spirits rose slightly as the thermometer on the wall climbed above thirty two degrees. Perhaps she wouldn't freeze to death, anyway. A kettle on top of the stove began to whistle cheerily.

"Come on Annie." Kent's voice broke into her thoughts. "The shower is ready and I'll hand a cup of hot chocolate and brandy in there to you."

"A shower?... Here?" she said.

Kent laughed. "Your face is a study," he said. "Yes, a shower... here. I pounded a pipe down into the ground to the water table and I pump water with an electric pump, run by my generator."

"But isn't that water awfully cold?" she asked, wearing a dubious expression on her face. "I remember how the creek felt – like ice water."

She shivered again at the memory.

"It'll be nice and warm, I promise you," he said. "Trust me, it runs through a propane fired hot water heater that heats it as fast as it runs through. It's a marvel of modern technology."

He took her hand, led her into the bathroom, and left her there.

She began to strip off her wet clothing. What a relief it was to get out of it. Her shirt and jeans, she threw in a heap on the floor. Her bra had just joined them, when Kent entered with a steaming mug, startling her.

Annie saw how his eyes caressed the thrusting mounds of her breasts and noticed her nipples beginning to stiffen in response to his gaze.

She felt a surge of panic... or was it excitement. Self-consciously she hid herself behind her towel, an all gone feeling swirling in the pit of her stomach.

His eyes dropped, as he handed her the mug, clearly appreciating the full curves of her calves and thighs, with a hungry expression that increased her agitation.

A hot wave of blood burned across her cheeks. "Please?" she pleaded, weakly.

Kent nodded and smiled, seeming to understand. Handing her a long terry cloth robe, he said, "Go ahead and get warmed up. Put on this robe when you're done."

The beat of hot water on her back was the ultimate luxury. It ran down over her body and legs, warming her, stimulating the flow of blood and drawing it to the surface. Soon, she warmed up enough to shiver. She had never been too cold to shiver before.

Greedily, she gulped the steaming chocolate with trembling hands. In the city, she had forgotten how wonderful such simple things could be. As the glow of warmth spread through her, she began to relax. The strong infusion of brandy spread its own brand of inner warmth.

She dawdled a bit longer in the shower, stalling for time.

He was going to want to make love to her now. Excitement and fear rose in her. Odd, how difficult it was to tell the difference between the excitement and the fear.

Resolutely, she turned off the shower and stepped out to towel herself off. As she dried, she looked for the toilet.

Strange. That fixture was missing. She would have to ask him about it. She slipped on the robe and belted it tightly around herself.

At the door, she paused, summoning her courage. She was going into the next room with a strange man and wearing only a robe.

She felt oddly unhappy as she realized that she had stranded herself in the midst of a real wilderness, at the mercy of the passions and appetites of a man she didn't even know.

Well, she had made her choice. She would just have to make the best of it. How did the old saying go? "You have made your own bed. Now, you have to lie in it."

The cabin, itself, was a disappointment, too. But maybe she could do something about that. She opened the door and marched into the main room, chin high, feigning a boldness that she didn't feel.

Kent smiled and asked, "Feel better?"

He grinned at her, boyishly. The fine laugh wrinkles, at the outer corners of his sparkling chocolate drop brown eyes, giving him an appealing, sexy, air of good humor.

The jagged scar, running across the left cheek of his strong, square face, made him appear romantic – piratical, or something.

Dangerously, he wore only a towel, wrapped around his waist. Beneath it, his calves bulged pleasingly with muscle, hairy and masculine. Below his left collar bone, Annie noticed a ragged edged, round scar.

Dark brown hair curled crisply on his chest, arrowing down to disappear beneath the towel. She trembled and looked away, glancing around the room.

The thermometer now said seventy five, she noticed. "I feel much better," she said. Then, hesitantly, added, "Kent, I couldn't find the toilet."

"It's in the outhouse across the yard. I'll walk out there with you, when you're ready," he replied. He drew her up beside the stove with him.

Annie's dismay grew. In her mind she pictured the ancient outhouse on her father's farm, still used occasionally by some of the farm hands, even though there was indoor plumbing in the house. It was dilapidated and reeked with foul odors.

Dimly she was aware of him saying, "It has been an eventful day, hasn't it Annie?"

She nodded.

He took her in his arms and his lips took hers aggressively. Stirred, she felt his hands slip inside her robe and begin to stroke her body. He cupped a breast, squeezing it gently, then began to stroke the nipple with his thumb.

Unhappiness and dismay reinforced the fear, the sense of strangeness, and the odd sensations surging through her belly. He was being completely insensitive. Couldn't he tell how unhappy and frightened she was? Didn't he care?

A great lump swelled in her throat. Tears welled in her eyes, spilled over, and began to run down her cheeks.

With a strangled sob, she stiffened and pushed at him. Shocked, Kent released her and stepped back.

He peered at her, a dismayed expression on his face, as the floodgates burst. Scalding tears rolled down her cheeks, accompanied by racking sobs.

She tried hard to stop, gulping back sobs. "What kind of wife am I being?" she asked herself. The question only made her sob harder.

Kent took her gently in his arms. "What is it Annie?" he asked, greatly concerned.

She nestled her head against him and struggled to speak past the great lump in her throat. "I... just... guess... that I... am over tired," she forced out, gulping and sobbing between words. More tears rolled down her cheeks.

She sobbed again – and wailed, "And... and... I just... I'm still a virgin... and I was frightened... and I realized, all of a sudden, that I don't really... know you..." It all came out in a rush.

Tears streamed down her cheeks, as she said more calmly, "And I was so frightened on the way here, and wet. I felt so stupid, almost drowning myself in knee deep water, 'cause I was too dumb to stand up. And, then, you laughed at me!... and – you never said anything about an outhouse before, in your letter."

She was feeling better already for having let it out.

Kent was holding her tight and kissing the tears from her cheeks. He really was a sensitive and caring man, after all.

Perhaps, if he was gentle it wouldn't be so bad. She sought the right mood – tried to feel sexy. It was part of the bargain, after all. And she had made the bargain with her eyes open.

She waited for him to start making love to her again.

He held her head against his shoulder and said, "I understand Annie. We don't need to rush. I'll give you a little time to get to know me better, before I take you to bed."

She cuddled into the warm, comforting protection of his arms. The tears slowed, then ceased. She sniffled and wiped her face with one sleeve of her damp robe.

"I didn't mention the outhouse," he said, "because I'm installing an indoor toilet. I intended to have it done before you got here, but I ran a day short of time. I'll have it working before tomorrow night."

Annie leaned back in his arms and looked up at him. She saw sadness in his eyes. Remorse sprang up in her breast.

"Oh, Kent!" she breathed. "I'm so sorry. I was thoughtless. I know that you tried hard to make this a happy day."

"It's ok, Annie, I understand – it has been an intense few days for you. The main thing is that I want you to be happy."

Kent settled her in the master bedroom that night and took the guest room for himself. Briefly, he looked in on her, tucking the quilt up beneath her chin, like Daddy used to do.

His kiss was warm against her lips but gently undemanding.

"Sleep in late tomorrow, sweetheart, you've had a hard day," he murmured.

Annie snuggled deep into the quilts, exhausted both physically and emotionally. She knew a moment of regret that he was not in her bed. She would have liked to cuddle up to him.

Mildly, she regretted not having gotten it over with. Now the dreaded first time still lay ahead of her.

"I wonder how Maggie is doing? Better than me, I hope," she said quietly into the darkness.

CHAPTER SIX

Annie was not in Maggie's thoughts at that moment. They were occupied with other things.

Maggie's red curls glowed, bright against her white pillow in the soft lamp light, as Blaine penetrated her for the third time this evening.

She moaned and surged against him, eagerly urging him on. Every nerve in her body, turgid with building pressure, demanded more.

The pressure built and built and built, to a sudden, explosive release.

She writhed in an agony of pleasure, her face wet with tears, then went limp with total satiation.

Aware of him still wetly filling her, embracing her and looking at her with concern, she clung to him.

"Please don't cry, Darling," he said, kissing tears from her cheeks.

She reassured him, drowsily, "I'm crying for joy. I love you my husband."

Suddenly, she was very tired... spent.

He withdrew, and lay beside her, pulling her head onto his shoulder, and turned off the lamp.

She snuggled tight against him, throwing an arm across his hard, flat stomach. A glow of happy satisfaction suffused her being.

This felt so right, as though she had been waiting for it all her life without knowing it. With a happy moan, she sought to snuggle even closer.

Then, her eyes dropped shut and she fell into a deep and dreamless sleep.

The morning sun shone through the curtains, open a crack in the center. It laid a golden path across Maggie's face, shining redly through her closed eyelids.

She stirred and knew contentment, as she found herself tightly enclosed in his arms. For the first time in her life, she had slept in the nude. She luxuriated in her sense of wickedness.

He was asleep, yet his maleness thrust against her demandingly. Apparently it led a life of its own. She giggled softly to herself.

Careful not to disturb him, she wriggled free and rose, crossing to the window.

Opening the curtain, she looked out. Miles of solitude rolled south from her viewpoint, framed in snow frosted spruce trees at the edge of the clearing.

Everything wore a mantle of purest gleaming white. And to the far south, ragged peaks clawed the sky, smoky blue in the distance and wearing their own caps of snow that faded, in places, into the little, puffy clouds scattered on the horizon.

What a gift of fortune! The Lord was good, she thought, to give her the rest of her life to live in such a place... and with such a man.

Unexpectedly, she was gathered into an embrace, and pulled back against him. He had crept up on her, undetected. She purred as he kissed her neck and let his hands stroke her lean belly, then rise to cup her breasts.

"Good morning, Mrs. Burns, my Love," he said, in a low whisper.

"Good morning to you, Sir," she said, in a saucy tone. "And who is this, that has come up behind me, making so free with my person."

"It had damn well better be your husband!" he growled, nipping fiercely at her right ear lobe.

In a stagy melodramatic tone, she replied, "La, Sir, I shall pray that it is." Then laughed. "I've been reading too many of those Regency romances.

They stood a moment, gazing out at the splendid vista. Then she said, "I'm eager to start my new life. What chores have you planned for us to do today?"

"None for several days," he replied. "This is our honeymoon. Later, there are potatoes to dig, other crops to harvest and can, and we must kill a moose for our winter meat."

"No chores, Sir? Well, then, let's get dressed and walk out to see my new country," she said.

"I might rather just keep you in bed all day," he said. He let one of his hands drop lower, trailing fire through her nerves.

Her belly muscles began to ripple spasmodically. "But I thought you said no chores?" she protested, playfully.

"Chores?" he said and snorted. "You look on this as a chore? Well, In that case, you are required to do one chore, to earn your walk."

He swept her up off her feet and carried her, laughing and kicking and squealing, to the bed where she simultaneously lost and won a joyous tussle.

They stood in a wooded gulch, hand in hand, watching a little waterfall froth over a six foot drop. The small pool at the bottom lay surrounded by snow frosted ferns.

Some of the blue mountains were framed in the mouth of the gulch.

"What mountains are those?" she asked.

He replied, "The Alaska Range. The largest, toward the right hand end of what you can see from the bedroom, is Denali. It's home to the Arctic Gods, according to native lore. The range runs more than three hundred miles, east to west, and rises to a little over twenty thousand feet."

Blaine led her on an exploration of the trails and thicket and she fell more and more in love with the land, and with her man. He was a natural man that belonged here.

Coming to the even rows of small trees, she asked, "Is this your Christmas tree farm?"

He nodded. His grin, she found, was infectious – she felt her own lips curling upwards at the corners, in answer.

"Pretty, aren't they?" he said. "Quite unlike our straggly shaped native trees. We think that we'll do well with them... most Christmas trees are imported from outside – Michigan, Montana, or where-ever, and that's expensive. So we should be able to beat their price and still make a nice profit."

Returning to the cabin, she lingered behind a moment, looking at the remnants of the garden, beneath its frosting of white. Stealthily, she gathered snow, warming it in her hands and making a tight, hard little snow ball.

Blaine's first hint of her treachery was the impact, as the snow ball exploded against the middle of his back.

He quickly regrouped his faculties and retaliated in kind and the air was filled with volleys of snow balls back and forth and merry shouts and laughter.

Blaine was losing the exchange, until he rushed her and scooped her up into his arms. In spite of her vigorous kicking and squirming, he carried her into the cabin. He kicked the door shut behind him and carried her on into the bedroom, where he changed the field of battle to one where he could win.

Three glorious days of honeymoon passed, days spent walking, building snowmen, laughing and sledding.

He taught her to fire the shotgun, after she begged him prettily, and took her grouse hunting. She brought down their dinner on the second day, in two bursts of flying feathers, and found it good.

"Somehow food that you've killed or grown yourself is more satisfying," Blaine reflected – and she understood exactly what he meant.

And there were the repeated bedroom tussles that she lost... and, in the losing, won.

On the evening of the third day, the noise of an engine droned distantly, growing louder as it approached and finally stopped before the cabin. Hurriedly, once they realized it was drawing closer, they sprang out of bed and pulled on their robes.

They rushed to the door and flung it open.

Kent got off the snow machine and stood up, just as they opened the cabin door, spilling yellow light in a long rectangle across the snow.

Blaine and Maggie stood in the doorway, looking out. Maggie's disheveled, red curls tumbled around her freckled face.

"Hi, old buddy," Blaine said. His tone was surprised. He waited expectantly for Kent to say something.

Maggie looked at him questioningly, raised an eyebrow at his continued silence, then asked, "Where's Annie?"

An expression of pure misery crossed Kent's face. He choked back a sob and said, gravely, "I had hoped that you would know."

He bowed his head and stood in silence.

CHAPTER SEVEN

Annie stirred, disturbed by a sunbeam slanting through the window to fall across her face. She stretched and luxuriated beneath the heavy quilts, warm and comfortable in her flannel night gown.

Still half asleep, she puzzled a moment. Where was she? Then she remembered. Yesterday had been her wedding day.

As Kent had tucked her in last night, he had told her to sleep late this morning. She must have, it looked like full day light out there.

Her glance strayed out the curtainless window to where spruce trees showed snow trimmed tops, sun lit golden against the vivid blue sky. Behind them rose rugged peaks frosted with white.

She examined her feelings. She felt well rested, she decided, not like sleeping any more. Her face flushed as she recalled the previous evening. She hoped that he didn't think her a fool and a hysteric. Regretfully, she thought that she had given him a hard time, not much of a wedding day. He deserved better and she had some amends to make.

Her watch lay on the bed stand. Picking it up, she saw that it read eleven o'clock.

"Oh!" she gasped, "so late."

Ruefully she said, "Now he's going to think that I'm a lazy thing, as well as hysterical and flighty."

She was tempted to pull on the robe and go in search of coffee immediately.

"No," she told herself. "I don't want to do anything to arouse him just now." She felt a faint surge of panic at the thought. "I still need a little time to settle in, before I'm really ready for that."

She got up and found that her suitcases stood neatly by the door, a thoughtful gesture. She swung them up onto the bed and threw them open. Swiftly she found her underwear and put it on.

Turning her attention back to the suitcases, she rummaged through them, deciding what to wear. From one, she extracted a cowboy shirt that she had purchased while shopping for her trousseau. She held it up against her and smiled. She and Maggie had had such fun on that shopping trip.

The shirt bore a colorful pattern of red, green and blue. Down the front ran ivory colored snaps. Putting it on, she looked in the mirror, smiled again, and said, "This will make me look pretty and cheerful for him."

Now she combed out her hair, then drew on her jeans and socks and padded out into the main room. There, a pot of coffee stood on a trivet atop the wood stove. Above it, a row of colorful mugs hung from hooks on the log beam.

Warmth radiated from the stove, and the pop and crackle of the leaping flames was a pleasing sound to her ears.

Having filled a mug, she put her back to the stove, savoring the warmth. She let her eyes wander as she sipped appreciatively. The strong, hot coffee warmed her belly.

The room was not so bad as she had thought. It had definite possibilities. She had just been gloomy and depressed the night before.

Its walls glowed with the homey warmth of mellow, golden, varnished spruce and the items hung on them were picturesque.

Over all, the room was clean and bright. All it needed was a woman's touch... ruffled curtains at the windows, bright towels by the sink, and a few bright knickknacks and pictures on the wall.

She would have to ask him for permission to buy the things she needed on their shopping trip. Asking permission would be hard, for she was used to doing as she pleased, but she had almost no money of her own.

So thinking, she examined the room more closely.

The yellow spruce logs that made up the wall reflected the light warmly, as did the knotty spruce boards of the roof that rose steeply above the beams of the open log ceiling.

It was a spacious room, thirty by thirty she guessed, furnished as a living room on one side. In the middle of that wall, near the sofa, a stone fireplace that rose to the ceiling lent an air of welcoming warmth. In it, too, a modest fire crackled, warming the room. It all had the air of a hunting lodge.

Pleased, she noted the shelves of books, rising alongside the fireplace. He was a reader, too... but, then, he had said so, she recalled. She discovered some old friends there on the shelves – Hemingway, Steinbeck and Howard Fast among them.

On the other side of the room she saw a country style, pine, dining room set, light in finish and bright. It stood in a corner illuminated by large, three pane windows. Beyond it, the kitchen was arranged along one wall. She wandered to the sink.

She looked out the window, above the sink, to see a wonderland of glistening white. It was beautiful, almost like a Currier and Ives print. Several grey-crested birds pecked busily at biscuit crumbs scattered on a spruce stump from which the snow had been swept. One cocked a bright eye at her inquisitively.

Under its blanket of fresh snow, the clearing rolled gently down to a creek that sparkled in the morning sun. Primeval forest lay beyond – towering, deep green spruce, with golden puffs of birch and cottonwood sprinkled among them.

She spun around, startled, as the door burst open behind her, with a bang.

Kent entered, slamming the door behind him and stomping his feet to clear them of snow. He wore engineers' boots, an open, blue, wool-lined denim jacket and a cowboy hat.

How rosy his cheeks were. He was a handsome devil and ruggedly manly. What was this odd sensation coiling within her?

"Good morning," he said heartily. He sounded cheerful but had a solemn look about him. "How are you feeling this beautiful morning?"

"Much better. I guess that there was nothing wrong with me that twelve hours sleep couldn't cure," she said and smiled warmly.

Would he give her a kiss? She found herself longing for one.

A grin crossed his face. "Please come sit down and have a cup of coffee with me," he said.

She saw that his sharp eyes had noted her suddenly rosy cheeks. Her ears burned, as she smiled, shyly, and nodded.

Obediently, she went to the stove, filled a mug for him and topped off her own. She took them to the table, where he had sat down astride a reversed chair, resting his chin on its high back.

With a tremulous little laugh, Annie said, "I have so much to learn. I don't even know how you like your coffee."

"Lots of sugar," he replied and pulled a ceramic sugar bowl to him, spooning three spoons of sugar into his mug. "Cream is over there in the propane refrigerator, if you want it," he added, gesturing at it.

"Thanks, but I take mine black," she replied, "Daddy always said that I was already sweet enough." She giggled, and heard a faint note of hysteria. What ever possessed me, to say a stupid thing like that? she thought. But she was pleased to see a faint grin flicker across his face.

The unbroken silence, as they sipped their coffee, was awkward. She desperately sought something else to say, anything, but drew a mental blank.

"I've been feeding my pets," he said.

"Your pets?" She looked at him inquiringly.

"Yes, those jay birds you were looking at. Camp robbers, we call them around here. They get quite tame...you'll be able to get them to eat out of your hand in a week or two, once they get to know you."

"Oh... they're cute." She didn't know what else to say. Wow, Annie, you're a real intelligent conversationalist, she congratulated herself, sarcastically.

After another lengthy silence, he said, "It's a wonderfully pretty day out there today. I'd like to take you for a walk after coffee, show you around my kingdom."

"I think that I would enjoy that," she answered and smiled brightly. "It does look like a lovely day."

More silence followed – and Kent fidgeted uncomfortably. The two strangers, now husband and wife, groped for something more to say, some way to break the ice.

Annie let her eyes wander, seeking inspiration. Finally, she broke the silence, saying, "I like the cabin so well, Kent...Would you mind, though, if I brightened it up some, added some woman's touches? I'd like to get you to buy me a sewing machine, some curtain material and a few wall hangings, when we go to town."

She held her breath, waiting his answer, for she had no idea of how generous or stingy he might be. It made her feel vulnerable, which somehow annoyed her and yet, strangely, pleased her, at the same time.

To her relief, a happy smile lit his features. At least the question hadn't made him angry.

"Awww, so you've decided to stay," he said happily.

She felt surprise. Did he have shy fears, just as she did? He seemed so strong and self sufficient.

"Of course I'm staying, Kent. I'm your wife. And I want to be a good one," she said. Impulsively she reached out and took his hand. "I had no thought of leaving and I'm sorry if I led you to think that I did."

His hand engulfed hers warmly. He gave it a little squeeze.

"I'm glad. You sure had me scared last night – scared that it was all over before it even started," he drawled trying, unsuccessfully, to conceal the depth of his feelings. He gazed into her eyes, and she saw a warm and generous spirit there in the chocolate depths.

She squeezed his hand warmly, to reassure him, and said, "I'm sorry. I'll grow to love this place – and you. I'm sure of it."

He cleared his throat. Gruffly, he said, "I have a couple of presents for you to open, before we go walking."

With that, he rose and crossed the room to open a cedar chest that stood next to the sofa. He dug two parcels from the chest and turned to her with them.

She had trailed him across the room, and now sat on the hearth where it projected from the fireplace. The flames leapt and crackled.

As he handed her the packages, his expression was nothing, if not bashful, and it stirred a feeling of tenderness toward him.

Excitedly, she tore open the wrappings of the first package and pulled out a pair of boots.

She pulled on the soft, furry boots, tucking in the legs of her jeans, and stood. They embraced her legs in warmth, nearly to the knee. The fur sparkled, as did her eyes.

"Those are Eskimo style boots, called mukluks," he informed her, beaming over her pleasure. "I had them made of beaver that I trapped myself."

"Here. Open this," he commanded, handing her the other package.

Ripping the paper from it, she opened the box, exposing a hat that appeared to be made from a whole little animal.

Kent placed it on her head and, taking her by the shoulders, turned her to face the mirror above the mantle. "It's black phase marten, what the Russians call sable," he murmured. "I caught it myself, too. Actually there are three of them in that hat... their hides are rather small."

She turned to him, eyes aglow. "You're making an Alaskan girl of me already," she said.

He leaned nearer. "The Belle of the Salchena Valley," he said admiringly. His breath was warm on her cheek and the pleasant, manly smell of his after shave filled her nostrils.

"Thank you, I love it," she breathed, offering him her lips.

Her arms went around his neck. He accepted her kiss gently, then began to warm as she lingered. His arms went around her and molded her against him.

The wave of tenderness that swept through her broke, as she felt his maleness grow hard against her. The fright seemed less, not a panic this time, yet it spoiled the mood.

She pulled her lips free and wriggled to loosen his hold, but remained in the circle of his arms.

Softly, she reminded him, "You did say that you'd give me a little time."

Regretfully, he replied, "Yes, I did, and I will... A little time." "– But a man can stand only so much, you know," he warned.

A small thrill of excitement tickled within her, not wholly unpleasant, but she subdued it.

"Come," he said. "Throw on a coat and I'll show you my land, your new home."

She went for her coat, shrugged into it, and went with him out the door. The crisp, dry, twenty degree air was refreshing. She breathed it in deeply, savoring the rich odors. The pleasant scent of wood smoke mingled with the smell of spruce and of autumn leaves in a heady perfume.

To her right, a deep trench emerged from under the cabin, angling sharply downward for, perhaps, a hundred yards... to end in a large square hole in the ground,lined with upright logs.

"What's that?" she asked.

"The drain field for the toilet, the pipes are just about all connected. Mainly I just need to hook it up inside. Course, I need to bury all this and smooth it over, once I'm done."

"And you dug it all by hand, so that I could have an inside toilet," she marvelled, noticing a sharp pointed shovel leaning against the cabin.

"That must have been a lot of work," she said, slowly realizing the magnitude of his wedding gift to her.

"It only took about a week," he said, in a gruff tone.

Kent reached out for her hand and she nestled it in his, warm and compliant. Holding it firmly, he led her past the several out buildings, and on past the garden, now mostly bare, but for the rows of potatoes.

Before they reached the creek, they turned and went on along a snowy path that wandered into the forest.

He stopped, leaning over a scarlet cranberry bush, snow frosted. "Look," he said, "how the sun shines through the crystals, like works of art."

At his prompting, she studied them, her eyes seeing the delicate magic of the individual snow flakes, no two alike. They stood out clearly against the deep red of the cranberry foliage.

As they went on through the glistening stillness of the forest, he called her attention to the tales written in the snow. Here, the tiny trail of a mouse, scurrying from one haven to the next. There, the hop marks of a snowshoe rabbit – hotly pursued by the running tracks of a fox. A ways further, crimson snow and bits of fur spoke of a tragic end to that tale, for the rabbit.

Kent read the stories to her, explaining how to distinguish the tracks of each animal, how to tell casually strolling tracks from running tracks. They went on down the trail, through a thick stand of brush.

Suddenly, he froze. "Look," he whispered, "Grouse, sitting so still. The silly things think that we can't see them."

Annie looked. She intently studied the part of the thicket he pointed at, but could'nt see them. She felt really foolish. "They're right," she said, "I can't see them."

Carefully he explained where they were, pointing, and suddenly, her perspective shifted. Now she could see them. They were crouched motionless, barely twenty feet away.

Kent motioned and they moved off quietly, careful to avoid scaring the birds. Hopefully, they would stay in the vicinity. Some of them would be on the dinner menu, perhaps Saturday or Sunday, he explained.

The path wound on through the forest. In the midst of a grove of birch, still crowned with gold, a rough bridge arched over the chuckling creek. Kent stopped to lean upon the rail.

Staring into the water, he said, "I'm not a church-goer, don't believe in them. But I *am* religious. Out here... this is my church. Listen, and you can hear His voice in the whisper of the wind and the swirl of the water."

Silently, Annie nodded and covered his hand with hers, as she stood staring into the water. She did hear something mystic. A warm glow suffused her, that he was sharing this with her.

"One day this week I'll bring you here fishing, and we can catch our dinner," Kent said. He straightened, took her hand and led her onward.

The trail looped around a stand of big spruce with neat piles of firewood stacked among them. "This is where I'm cutting this winter's wood," he explained, "I'll haul it in on my snow machine sled as we need it."

Further along, the trail swung back across the creek. There was no bridge here. He showed her how to balance on rocks that protruded from a shallow place in the creek, and hop across to the other bank.

Annie squealed and giggled, as she teetered across, feeling that she would fall in at any moment. It was something like the feeling of riding a rollercoaster – a delicious sense of danger, yet the secure knowledge that nothing could go too seriously wrong. At worst, a wetting, and she had already survived one of those, with no ill effect.

As they re-entered the home clearing, she saw that large patches of snow had gone, and the rest was melting rapidly.

"Oh," she pouted. "The lovely snow is leaving."

Kent laughed. "Trust me, you will have had plenty of snow by May. The snow will stick before the end of September. Then it will be here all winter – at least seven long months."

By the time they returned to the cabin, several hours had fled and it was nearing dinner time. She had had no breakfast either, as her clamoring stomach reminded her. For that matter, she had not eaten well for several days. She had been too nervous and excited.

Kent cooked for her – moose steak, pounded and rolled in flour and spices, and fried in butter. It was delicious, as were the biscuits and beans he served with it.

During the meal, he entertained her with stories of the animals that shared their country. His enthusiasm was infectious and she thrilled to the adventure of her new life in this strange land.

She must become a full partner in his life and take up her wifely duties, sharing the chores.

"Please get me up when you get up tomorrow morning," she said. "I want to start cooking your meals. I can cook, you know."

Annie was clearing the table, planning to wash the dishes. As she worked, she asked, "What are your plans for the next few days?"

Kent said, "Well, first, I plan to finish the indoor toilet, that'll probably be an all day project. Then, next day, I want to go shoot a moose. You remember, I pointed out signs of a bull hanging around, back there where we crossed the creek. They like to eat the willow brush that grows so thick along that stretch. Then I'll have to cut up the moose, after hanging it in the shop. It'll take me several days, because I want to freeze some of it and can the rest. Maybe I'll make one crock of corned moose... and a little jerky."

He reflected a moment, then drawled, "I had planned for you to spend the day tomorrow unpacking your boxes." He pointed to the stack at the guest room door. "I reckoned it would take you a day to get them sorted out and put away."

For a moment, he appeared to ponder. Then he continued, "The next day, I figured on you helping me with the cutting up and canning of the meat – then, after that, I wanted to turn the ground and have you pick up the potatoes and store them."

A red flash of anger burned across her vision. "I've been accustomed to planning my own day, thank you," she exclaimed, in a voice that trembled with anger.

"Annie, I think it's only right that you should share in the chores," he said patiently. A surprised look had appeared on his face.

"Oh! Implying that I'm lazy? I intend to help with the chores but I want you to discuss it with me, not give me orders!" she snapped. She hadn't suspected that he could be such a tyrant, though she should have from his bossy tone yesterday.

"Well, I guess that we can discuss things – but, as to the final say... well, there is room for only one captain on a ship, and only one decision maker in a family," he rejoined. He was speaking in an infuriatingly calm and reasonable tone of voice.

Her father had always spoken to Mom like that, with a calm assurance that she would do just as she was told. Annie had sometimes resented that. Certainly, Annie herself was accustomed to being independent. She was not about to start taking orders now.

Angry tears rose to her eyes. She slammed the stack of plates and silver into the sink, with a satisfying crash.

"Leave the dishes, I'll do them in the morning," she choked out. Tears stung her eyes. – Oh no, he was going to think that she was a little ninny that did nothing but cry all the time. Fat lot of good that would do her attempt to take a strong stand. She tried to blink back the tears.

"Annie, we're just having a discussion. Why are you crying?" he asked.

Now the tears began to roll down her cheeks. "I don't know," she sobbed, angrily. If only he would yell at her, so that she could fight back. Damn him! It was unfair of him to be so calm and reasonable.

Kent had a peculiar expression on his face, uncertain. He said nothing, gazing at her in silence.

"Oh! If you don't understand, I can't tell you. You... you, man!" she sobbed and rushed into the bedroom, slamming the door behind her.

Kent sighed, rolling his eyes upwards. "Oh, Lord, help me. What have I gotten myself into?" he muttered. Shaking his head, he went to the sink and began to wash the dishes, mumbling to himself.

As she settled for the night, Annie grimly vowed to fight. She would not be a subservient little wimp. An equal partnership in this marriage was what she sought, and she meant to have it.

Next morning she woke to the rattle of wood being put into the stove. An aroma of perking coffee wafted temptingly through the crack of the door, which had come slightly ajar.

It's time to go on the offensive, she told herself, as she got up and slipped on her robe, belting it firmly. Wasn't it possible to be a good wife and have a good marriage, without being a slave?

Quickly, she ran a comb through her hair, letting it flow softly about her face and fall to her shoulders. A splash of white shoulders in her palm, went on as a dab behind each ear and onto the v at the base of her throat.

She marched determinedly into the main room.

Kent, in his long johns, turned toward her. "Good morning," he greeted her, his manner civil but a little cool.

She smiled sweetly. Briefly, as she marched past him to the kitchen area, she paused to let her lips linger momentarily on his.

Glancing back, as she reached the refrigerator, she caught a bemused look on his face.

"What would you like for breakfast?" she asked cheerfully. Not waiting for a response, she opened the refrigerator door. "Here's some bacon, eggs... I don't see any bread."

"No," he replied, "I used it all up. I had meant to bake some more."

"Bacon and eggs then?" she asked.

He nodded. Pulling up a chair, he sat at the table.

As she got out the food, she said briskly, "Well, then, I think that I'll take today, as you suggested, to unpack and get settled in. Tomorrow, I want to go hunting with you. Moose hunting is an experience that I have looked forward to and I don't want to miss. The next day, I'll bake bread and cinnamon rolls and a pie... maybe some cookies."

She arranged bacon in the pan, as she continued, "You said that you've got more wood to cut and split?"

"Yes," he said, slowly, a wondering expression on his face. "We'll need about twenty cords to make it through the winter – I've only got about fifteen or sixteen split and stacked. And I always like to have extra. It's hard to get around for more, if I run short after it's already snowed twelve feet."

"Cords?" she asked.

"That's how we measure wood. A cord is a stack four feet wide, four feet high and eight feet long. The stove burns up a lot of wood when it gets fifty or sixty below outside."

She turned and crossed the room, to give him a hug from behind, whispering in his ear, "Why don't you be a dear – work on your wood cutting after we kill the moose, then I'll help you with the meat the next day?"

Leaving a kiss on his cheek, she turned back to her cooking. Mother always said that you catch more flies with honey than with vinegar. Come to think of it, mother did seem to get her way most of the time.

A little dazed looking, he agreed, "Yes, I guess that I could do that. But I do want to have you practice shooting this afternoon."

Annie smiled, another meltingly sweet smile, "Fine," she said, "I'll have lunch for you at one." He seemed to be responding well. Maybe she was on to something here.

"Do you have a rifle that I can use?" she asked.

"Sure do," he replied, "I have two of them." He got up and took one down from the wall. "You can use this one."

She smiled. "I'll bet that you are a good shot with it," she said.

"You bet... I can hit a fly with it," he drawled.

"Now you're teasing me."

His eyes turned to the kitchen window, where a fly buzzed noisily. With quick motions, he jumped up, and crushed the little creature with the butt of the rifle. "There," he said, eyes mischievous, as he sat back down.

"Kent! That was awful." She wiped the little crushed corpse and the goo off the window frame.

"Well, if you don't kill them, you are overrun with flies, before you know it."

"I meant the pun was awful," she said, "and you know it." Then she giggled. "I was shocked, when you pulled that on me. I can see I'm going to have to keep a careful eye on you."

She poured them each a cup of coffee, stirring three teaspoons of sugar into his cup.

She set his cup before him on the table, returning in a few moments with two plates of bacon and eggs.

"Kent?" she said. She lifted a slice of bacon to her mouth.

He raised his eyes from his plate. They held a tender glow, as they swept her face, that turned to a hungry look as they dropped lower.

A hot flush burned across her cheeks, as she became aware of how her robe had drooped open exposing her breasts.They were outlined clearly by the thin, clinging night gown. His gaze felt like a physical caress and roused a sweet turmoil in her blood.

Hastily drawing her robe closed, she said, "Dear, you never answered my question yesterday."

His eyes returned to her face. "What question was that, sweetheart?" he asked.

Her spirit trembled. Would he be generous with her, or had he evaded her question out of a mean stinginess?

He noticed her hesitation and an impatient frown crossed his face, like a small thunder cloud.

Seeing that, she summoned her nerve, and spoke. She said, "I asked if you would buy me a sewing machine and some material. I'd like to make curtains and things to give a wife's touch to the cabin."

Before he could reply, she hastened to add, "I'm coming to you nearly penniless, you know, for our jobs in the city didn't pay enough to allow for saving. I spent most of what little I had on my trousseau."

A warm smile spread across his face and was reflected in his eyes. She found herself wearing a smile in answer. He was so darned appealing when he smiled.

"Don't fret, Darling Annie," he said earnestly. "I'll buy the sewing machine and we can shop together for curtain material and I'll buy it."

Then, Kent grinned. He said, "A woman should have some money of her own, that she can spend without having to ask permission. I intend to give you an allowance of a hundred dollars a month for mad money."

Allowance? The term caused a curiously weak and dependent feeling, treacherously not unpleasant.

As she found herself going into his arms, she murmured, "Dear Kent, thank you for having a generous spirit."

She turned up her face and his lips seemed to float down to meet hers.

The kiss started out firmly and grew warmer as he sucked and nibbled at her lower lip. His tongue probed. What was happening felt right. There was excitement, but no fear.

As he continued to kiss her, his hands undid the buttons down the front of her nightie. He scooped out her breasts, groaning as he discovered that their rosy, virginal nipples were already stiffened.

She moaned as his tongue and lips began their assault. He circled a nipple with the tip of his tongue, licking delicately.Gentle sucking was followed by delicate nips.

Yes! she thought, her excitement flooding her and crying for more. Now!

Suddenly, unexpectedly, he released her. A harsh groan broke from him as he stepped back.

He said, "I'm sorry, Annie. I know, I promised you more time. But it's hard."

He was breathing heavily and there was a great lump in the front of his long john pants.

Annie sobbed in frustration.

Misunderstanding her sob, he spun about and stalked to his room, calling back to say, "I'd better get dressed and get busy. I won't let that happen again until you are ready." He disappeared through the door.

Shaken, she stood a moment, then pulled her robe about her and trailed into her room.

She gazed wonderingly into the mirror as she traced her lips with a shaking finger and touched her aching, unfulfilled breasts. Shadows shifted in the depths of her green eyes.

In the next room, Kent groaned. His tension-filled groin throbbed. She would have gone along with him, damn it, he knew she would have. But he wanted her first time to be right, something she desired, rather than a command performance. He would have to control himself more carefully.

Both dressed moodily and started about their chores.

Later, Annie smiled as she arranged her Teddy bear and doll among her perfumes and cosmetics on top of the dresser. They were her only memento of her childhood, except for the photograph of her father and mother. She brushed angrily at a tear as she placed their photograph on the dresser.

"Give me a clue, Mom," she whispered, "What should I do next?" But, of course, there was no answer.

The sound of hammering and occasional swearing came from the bathroom at the back of the cabin. Kent was finishing up the toilet. He had promised that it would be working by evening.

She smiled tenderly. He was a dear, considerate man.

Actually the outhouse hadn't been that bad, clean and neat, with a not unpleasant medicinal odor. But it would be nice not to have to go outdoors through the cold, especially when it got down to fifty and sixty below.

A box jarred off the dresser, spilling loose sheets of paper. She gathered them up, then stopped to read one, then another. They were poems, by Kent, quite good ones. One, in particular, caught her eye:

TROPIC DAWN

Stretching far to either side, in tropic pre-dawn grey,
foaming surf outlined in white, the curving beach, Kihei.
I stepped into the surging warmth, it broke with hollow boom.
Black against the morning grey, I saw Ka-hoo-la-we loom.
Against the slowly greying sky, the horizon was stark and black.
Sparkling night lights on the coast, from the water reflected back.
I turned to face toward Maui now,
warm surf surged round my knees.
Lovely, exotic, tropic palms, whispered in the breeze –
every fiber of every frond, silhouetted clear and stark.
A wash of pink grew across the sky, to slowly banish dark.
Ha-le-ak-ala wore a rosy crown, pink puffs of cloud were west.
Amongst a spreading golden glow, the sun rose from its rest.

The imagery called to her. She had dreamed occasionally of going to Hawaii. Now he was going to take her there. Obviously, he had been there before and loved it. She felt proud of her husband and stimulated by this further evidence of his sensitivity. She moaned again, as she recalled the intensity of his uncompleted love making this morning.

As she continued unpacking, she mused. She would have to make it clear to him that she was ready, but how? She couldn't just come right out and tell him. A hot blush scorched her cheeks.

Near evening, as the sun neared the western peaks, Kent sought her out.

She straightened from the last box, which she had just opened, and stretched and groaned. Her back ached from stooping over all day.

Kent looked sympathetic and brushed his lips across hers, leaving a glowing tingle.

"Leave that 'til tomorrow, sweetheart," he said. Grasping her hand, he led her to the bathroom. There he grinned proudly as he pulled the handle of the toilet and caused a rushing noise of water as it flushed.

"See, Annie, one toilet as promised. The water comes out of that thirty gallon tank," he gestured at it, "If it runs out, just flip the pump on with this switch. – But now, I still want to have you practice shooting the shotgun. I know you said you can handle rifles, but it's important to be able to shoot the shotgun, too."

He led her back through the cabin, and out onto the porch.

A long barreled gun leaned against the rail, black and deadly looking.

Annie looked at Kent appealingly. She protested, "Kent... I used to hunt rabbits and birds with a twenty-two and I want to shoot a moose with the big rifle... but shotguns scare me, especially that big one. I'm afraid that it'll kick the stuffings out of me. Do I really have to shoot it?"

Surely he wouldn't be such a brute as to make her shoot it when he could see that it frightened her.

He spoke in a firm voice. "There are bears and wolves in this country. You need to know how to protect yourself, if you go out in the forest alone. The shotgun is much more effective as a defense weapon at short range. It'll knock a bear on his butt immediately, where a rifle might not."

He thrust the shotgun at her. "Here," he said. "Take it."

"You shoot it first," she begged, cringing.

He gazed at her, consideringly. "All right," he said. "Watch this." He broke open the barrel and inserted two shot shells. The gun swept up to his shoulder and the barrel pointed at a young paper bark birch, about two inches in diameter, at the near edge of the clearing.

He said, "It won't hurt you, as long as you hold it tight against your shoulder and brace yourself."

There was a deafening boom and the tree swayed and fell, blown in half by the blast.

Annie flinched. Without pity, Kent handed her the gun.Firmly, he said, "I fired the right barrel, you cock the hammer and fire the left. Shoot that next tree." He pointed at another two or three inch diameter birch.

Her lower lip protruded and trembled. She blinked back threatened tears as she took the gun. Trembling, she cocked the hammer, and raised the gun to her shoulder. This was really mean of him.

"Remember, hold it firm against your shoulder," he ordered.

There was that tone of voice again, giving her orders. Anger overrode her fear. She pointed the gun at the tree, squeezed her eyes tight closed, and jerked the trigger. There was a deafening boom, and the gun pushed back strongly against her shoulder.

She opened her eyes, in time to see the second tree totter and fall.

As tender and sore as her shoulder felt, she was certain that it would be black and blue in the morning. Gently feeling it with her hand, she winced.

Kent held out two more shells. He said, "Now show me how to load it."

Her eyes blazed with indignation. She spluttered, "I already shot it and I did good. You can't make me shoot it again, you brute."

He started to laugh.

Enraged, she looked at him defiantly. He was laughing at her again.

He always found her distress amusing. How could she have ever thought him to be sensitive and considerate? It was obviously just an act he put on, when it suited him.

"You don't have to shoot it again tonight, Sweetheart," he explained. His manner was infuriatingly patient. "But I want you to make a habit of always keeping it loaded, in case you need it in a hurry... And, Sweetheart," he ordered, "never leave the clearing without the gun!"

Burning resentment welled up at his domineering tone. She fought back stinging tears, determined not to give him the satisfaction. In silence, she took the shells and loaded them into the gun. She thrust it at him and turned to walk into the house.

She was putting dinner on the table when he came in.

As they ate in silence, Kent cast questioning glances at her. He started to speak but thought better of it.

Finally, shuffling his feet, he cleared his throat. He said, "I made you shoot the shotgun because I love you and don't want you to be eaten by a bear."

She looked sideways at him from beneath lowered brows. "You made me shoot the shotgun because you are a bully!" she snapped.

Her chair scraped as she pushed it back and ran to her room, so that he would not see her tears.

In her bed, she knew that she had been wrong and that he had her welfare at heart. But he was so bossy. She would make amends in the morning, somehow.

He looked so stricken when I rushed out of the room, she thought, with a giggle. His shocked look floated in her mind's eye.

Exhausted, she slept the sleep of the just. It seemed that the night passed in the blink of an eye.

Groggily, she stirred, then sat up, when she noticed the first grey hint of light out the window. "It's too dark to see to shoot," she told herself, "but I can stoke the stove and make a pot of coffee. I'll get ready to go hunting."

She got her rifle down, from where it hung on the wall, and checked it again, as she sat at the table sipping coffee in the light of a kerosene lantern. It was loaded, ready to go. The crackling fire took the chill of the night from the room.

At four-thirty, she checked on Kent, who still slumbered peacefully. She'd surprise him by killing the moose herself. After all, she had done well with the twenty-two on rabbits, this rifle would be no different, and the target was much bigger.

Refilling her mug with coffee, she took up the rifle and stepped outside, marking in her mind the way to the section of the creek where the bull's tracks had been.

She closed the door silently behind her, and stopped for a few minutes to let her eyes become accustomed to the dusky predawn darkness. It was cold and crisp. Suddenly, it grew brighter and she gazed, spellbound, sucking in her breath, in a gasp. The pale light was not from the sun. It was nowhere near rising.

Above her, a many layered, rippling, ghostly green banner wavered – dancing, gauzy, against a backdrop of velvet black.

Hard, white points of twinkling light, pierced the velvet curtain of the Arctic night. And across the pole star, the darkest night, a wavering veil of shimmering red faded into being, with a hissing crackle.

The display of Aurora lasted, perhaps, fifteen minutes, then faded, to vanish like a puff of smoke. All was dark, but for the dim star light.

She sipped her coffee, then crept slowly toward the creek, trying to move as silently as a ghost, not stepping on any twigs, or brushing against any branches.

Upon arriving at the bank, just next to the deformed spruce she had noted as a landmark, she sank to the ground, her back against the tree. A low bush before her broke her outline, to avoid alarming any animals.

It was still too dark to see across the creek. She sipped again at her coffee and shivered, peering tensely into the darkness, her ears alert.

Every sound registered on her consciousness, alert for moose and fearing for bear. She reflected that fear certainly does sharpen the senses.

The water splashed and gurgled, rolling over the smooth rocks of the creek bed. Shards of ice tinkled, along the bank.

Now the trees and brush on the opposite bank were becoming visible, through the light fog hanging on the creek, and a gleam reflected from the water.

She drank the last of the coffee and set down the cup, wishing that she had brought a biscuit or something to chew on. She debated going back for one. But no, this was the time of day for the moose to be stirring. She didn't want to miss him.

Again, she shivered in the early morning chill. A tinge of delicate lime green, edged with pale peach, painted the horizon.

What beauty I have seen tonight, she thought, living in cities deprives us of so much.

Early rising birds began to twitter. Across the creek a squirrel scolded. The peach color intensified, painting the bottoms of scudding clouds.

A distinct series of splashes across and up river caught her attention. SPLASH... pause... SPLASH SPLASH, long pause.

She peered intently in the direction of the sound. "Let it be a bull moose," she asked – Only the bull moose were legal game – "Don't let it be a cow, or worse, a bear."

SPLASH... pause... SPLASH, SPLASH. The first golden rays of the rising sun struck her and the fog began to lift.

From the vapors, he suddenly appeared. Wraith like at first, then looming big and solid, an enormous expanse of horn striking awe into her. When measured, it would be found that the horns spanned sixty-two inches across and stood four feet above the top of the bull's head.

He was big and black, majestic. She noticed a wet, sweaty, weedy smell. At the fringe of her awareness, some ducks flew over, quacking.

Frozen, she watched him, forgetting the rifle in her hands. Then the moose sensed her – turned to look in her direction. Vapor jetted from his nostrils as he snorted, a loud whoof. He shook his horns. Trembling, she raised the rifle to her shoulder. Her heart was hammering so hard she feared a heart attack and her mouth was dry as cotton.

"Steady, Annie," she told herself, "Hold your breath. Center the cross hairs of the scope just behind his shoulder." The scope filled with black hair. It wobbled and shook, as she breathed heavily.

She had to lower the rifle a moment. Forcing herself to be steady, she took several deep breaths. Time stopped as she raised the rifle again and held her breath while aiming it.

"Squeeze the trigger, don't pull. It should be a surprise when it goes off," she chanted the litany. BOOM. The rifle spoke, the recoil pressing her back. The moose jerked and stood motionless.

"No, damn it, I can't have missed," she swore. Her heart pounding, she aimed again.

BOOM... BOOM... BOOM! The rifle spoke with authority. This time, the bull crumpled and fell down. Ringing echoes rolled back from the surrounding hills. She sniffed the exhilarating scent of burned powder. Her pulse thundered within her and her ears rang.

She reloaded and watched the massive corpse tensely for any movement. The huge horns projected five feet into the air.

After a few more minutes, she concluded that he was dead. She ran back toward the cabin to find Kent running across the clearing, wearing only his long john pants. He was running barefoot through the frost and patches of snow and carried his shotgun in his right hand.

"Oh, Kent," she shouted, "I got a big bull. We'll have plenty of winter meat." They swept into each others arms and danced an impromptu jig of jubilation.

"You're going to be a real sourdough!" he exclaimed, joyfully. "And here I was, still slug a-bed. Let me get dressed and grab the camera. Then we better get the insides out of him and get him quartered, so the meat can cool and not sour."

As he dressed, she gathered up the knives and a sharpener.

She swung down the path to the bank beside him, a light bounce to her step, to match the light happy feeling in her heart.

Moments later she was beside the massive corpse, standing silent a moment to admire the magnificent bull. She joined Kent, as he reverently thanked the bull for the gift of his life, a gift that would allow them to eat well this winter.

Proudly, she posed, grasping the rifle and the massive horns, as Kent preserved this triumph in his camera for posterity.

Leaning over, Kent worked his first knife through the tough neck hide and cut the bull's throat. Gallons of hot blood spurted onto the thirsty gravel, steaming in the lingering morning chill.

Her nostrils twitched at the strong scent of the blood and the lingering odor of burnt powder. Less strong, she smelled the pleasant odor of moldering autumn leaves... wet now with melting frost.

The sun was fully up by now and the chill was beginning to vanish, as was the frost on the stones, steaming away from the touch of sun beams. She raised her face to the golden ball, with the unconscious worshipfulness of a true Arctic denizen.

"Now the fun is over and the work begins," Kent said, grinning broadly. He fastened a strong rope to the bull's left front and rear legs. Then she helped as he hauled these ropes about two strong trees on the fringe of the gravel bar, pulling the moose onto his back, his legs spraddled.

With a fresh knife, the old one was dulled by contact with the coarse moose hair, he split the skin and flesh from the center of the throat down the center of the chest and belly.

"There'll be well over seven hundred pounds of meat on him," Kent gloated.

Then taking out the chain saw, he sawed through the rib cage, splitting the breast bone. Their hands and arms grew slippery with a thick coating of blood, clear to the elbows. Her jeans legs also became uncomfortably soaked and slimy with blood the saw threw on them.

A swarm of hungry gnats, attracted by the smell, attacked her. She couldn't swat them, not wanting to spread blood all over the rest of her.

Kent noticed her dilemma, and laughed. "No-see-ums, they call them," he grunted, "Damn – they may be small, but I see-um, feel-um too."

She laughed.

Grasping the esophagus, she laboriously drew the entrails from the moose and salvaged the heart and liver into a bucket she had brought for the purpose. This was not much different than when they had butchered hogs, back on the farm.

That done, they left the moose spread open to cool, and washed their hands, arms and pants legs in the river – and sank to a downed log for a well earned rest.

A bit later, after the moose had been quartered, Kent brought back the three wheeler. With its help, the moose was soon hauled back to the shop, hung, and skinned. Liver and onions was the menu that evening... and good home made kraut from Kent's crock in the pantry.

That night, again, she collapsed into a deep sleep, too exhausted for thought.

CHAPTER EIGHT

Another morning came, the third morning of their married life, a clear, golden autumn day.

Kent walked sleepily out into the main room to stoke the stove, and halted abruptly, obviously surprised to find that Annie was there before him.

Green eyes and hair like amber honey shone above a bewitchingly sweet smile. A tantalizing odor wafted to his nostrils.

What was she doing already up? She had had a hard day yesterday. The vision, dressed in a lime green and white checked dress and lacy apron, drifted to him. Taking his face in both hands, she rose on tiptoe and kissed him.

He was engulfed in a cloud of piquant scent from her perfume.

She retreated to the kitchen area, turning something in the frying pan with a spatula.

He broke free of his daze and said, "Mmm! What have I done to deserve this? It's wonderful. You'd better be careful, I could get used to this pretty easy."

Appreciatively, his eyes followed the swelling curves of the dress. A hunger stirred deep within. "You are gorgeous, sweetheart.

Annie giggled. "I'm so happy over getting the moose that I decided to pamper you," she said. "I'm making you a cheese omelette. And later I'll bring a picnic lunch to you where you are cutting wood."

An air of sexuality radiated from her that was in a fair way to driving him mad, but she was already up and dressed. Maybe it was a matter to explore further this evening.

"I wrote a poem about your moose last night, after you had gone to bed," he said, "Would you like to hear it?"

"I sure would," she replied, with a melting look. "I saw your other poems when I was unpacking. They're very good, especially Tropic Dawn – I had dreamed of going to Hawaii some day."

"We'll go there, soon... to Kihei, it's my favorite spot; miles of beaches, one after another, usually with hardly anyone on them. And the pocket of ocean, cupped in a protected bowl between Maui, Kahoolawe, Lanai and Molokai, it is tranquil. The whole thing is great – sun, surf, sand and palm trees."

"It sounds heavenly," she breathed.

He grinned and said, "Of course, I do want to take you to Waikiki, too, for a few days. It's something else... the party goes on twenty-four hours a day. And I want to show you the pineapple plantation, the Polynesian Culture Center – and take you to a luuau. Oh, we'll have a ball."

"Darling... Kent, it sounds great. But, about your poems, have you sent them to a publisher? If not, you should."

"No," he replied, "They are just something that I do for my own enjoyment. I have never considered them good enough to be published." He cleared his throat. "But let me read this new one. It's for you."

ARCTIC HUNTRESS' DAY

Amongst cottonwood's great golden puffs,
mixed with deep green spruce;
are scattered, brilliant, crimson strokes,
leaves of the currant bush.
Warm golden rays, fall on the rock,
frost vanishes as steam.
Frost sharpened blow, the scents of fall,
perfuming the faintest breeze.
She crouches there, beside the stream,

with bated breath keeps watch.
A black ghost appears, in the morning mist,
from nowhere, as in a dream.
With widened eyes, and nostrils flared,
blood surging, hot in her veins,
she lifts her rifle, holds it tight.
It speaks, a crashing boom.
Mighty horns jerk up, and freeze,
then fall, and disappear.
She leaps, and runs, to the brush,
she parts it, and she sees.
She turns and calls in a high sweet voice,
"A big one, and he's dead!"
I see her strut, coming back,
across the broken ground.
At home that night, the meat was hung.
The stars stood crisp and bright.
Her hand crept snuggling, into mine,
in the still of night.
Ruddy fire light flickered, as we sat,
well content with the day, and our life.

"You did that for me," she breathed, coming to him. Soft and sweet, her lips found his.

The omelette and fried potatoes were warm in Kent's belly as he rode off on the three-wheeler, chain saw, gas and tools strapped on behind.

A kiss tingled warmly on his lips and accounted for the hammering of his pulse. Yes, maybe tonight would be the night.

Annie watched him go from the kitchen window. What a fine looking man, she thought, stalwart in his jeans and boots, his stetson tilted back at a jaunty angle. She would have to persuade him to submit his poetry, see if any one would publish it.

He looked back with a grin and waved, before he disappeared into the forest.

The morning sped by as she baked bread, pies and cookies, fixing a lunch of fried chicken, deviled eggs, bread and butter pickles and potato salad in between her baking projects.

As she unpacked the last of the boxes she had shipped from the city and put the contents neatly away, Annie found herself contentedly humming a little tune.

Filled with a warm, satisfying sense of accomplishment, she glanced at the clock. Shocked, she saw that the clock read twelve o'clock – Noon.

She swiftly packed a hamper with the lunch and a thermos of hot coffee, putting in cups and napkins. She filled a paper bag with cookies, warm from the oven. No room for them in the hamper, not unless she crushed them. Oh well, she would just carry them in her other hand.

Just as she was about to leave, her gaze fell upon the shotgun, where it hung on the wall. He had said not to leave the clearing without it. But it would be hard to carry, with the other things she already had.

"Oh pooh! The bossy thing," she thought rebelliously, "he was just asserting his authority. There are no bears around here, and they wouldn't hurt me anyway."

It was only a short distance to the woodlot. She shrugged off the thought and stepped out the door, picnic basket in one hand and bag of cookies in the other.

The warm September afternoon sun had melted away the morning frost. It lay warm and golden across her face.

A saucy squirrel scolded at her from the safety of a spruce tree at the edge of the clearing, flirting its tail. She smiled. Pompous little creature.

Annie started off down the winding path and into the golden lit forest.

Her man would be pleased with the lunch. Thought of her man brought a smile to her face. 'My man'... magic words. She did want to please him.

The gold crowned grove of birch came into sight. She entered it and stepped out onto the bridge. There, she paused, looking into the crystal clear water.

Sunlight glistened from the surface. In the depths, a motion caught her eye. A fish... several fish. Arctic Grayling.

They were beautiful, with their large dorsal sails and colored sides flashing blue and green. The water rippled smoothly across the pool above the bridge.

The smooth flow of the water was broken as a grayling rose to pick a struggling fly from the surface... lunch. Concentric ripples spread, then faded. Moments later, another rose to eat another drifting bug, then returned to his station.

A sense of quiet contentment enveloped her. What a lovely peaceful place to live.

The sound of the saw was quite close now. Kent was hard at work. He must be just beyond the edge of the birch grove. Eagerly Annie hastened down the path, through the transition zone where the forest faded from birch back to spruce.

There he was. She saw him now with a glad eye. Did he see her? she wondered.

In the clearing ahead, Kent was bent over, sawing a downed tree trunk into stove-length pieces. His red hat stood out against the yellows, greens and browns of the forest. She caught his eye and waved happily.

The sound of the saw stopped, as he straightened, grinning broadly, and waved back to her.

Eagerly, she hastened forward.

Then Annie halted, her eye caught by the barest flicker of motion in the forest. She stared intently. Almost, she was convinced that she had imagined it. But no, there it was again.

Something large and black moved – there, off to the right.

Her pulse raced with the beginnings of alarm.

She peered through the underbrush. What was it? There... yes

definitely an animal.

It was a grizzly bear, just as Kent had warned. Why hadn't she brought the gun? There was the distinctive hump, the massive head. The smell of the bear reached her, a heavy mixture of strong sweat, rotten salmon, and skunk-like musk.

A chill ran up her spine and her hair bristled, trying to stand erect. She felt her heart thundering.

Should she run? Her legs seemed frozen. Her breath came in shallow, dry gasps. Why hadn't she listened to him? Dimly, she became aware of the sound of someone screaming. Who was that screaming? Was it her? It was!

For frozen moments she and the bear looked at each other. It seemed hours. Their eyes locked. She stared into the depths.

Pure, evil rage crossed the bear's face, making him look like a devil. The skin on his nose wrinkled and his eyes narrowed, as he bared his fangs in a snarl. The muscles of his forelegs bunched and his shoulders rippled as he tensed to spring.

"Oh God! Don't let me die this way," Annie prayed fervently. Her dry tongue rasped her lips.

Suddenly, the bear flinched back, confused by Kent's running arrival on the scene to stand between her and the bear.

"Keep behind me," Kent shouted. Two gun shots blasted out, deafeningly. Kent was firing over the bear's head.

The bear stood erect and roared a challenge. His forepaws were spread wide. He took a ponderous step forward, and another, massive and towering.

Her heart was going to burst. It hammered against her ribs. Pungent, burnt gun powder filled her nostrils, drowning out the vile odor of the bear. Her ears rang.

By now the bear stood only twenty feet from Kent – but Kent stood his ground and fired another shot over the bear's head.

"Get!" he shouted. "Don't make me kill you. Go on, get."

The bear flinched from the muzzle blast. Then, unhurriedly, it dropped to all fours, turned, and shuffled off into the forest. Kent watched him go, then turned to Annie.

She set down the hamper and bag that she had clutched tightly throughout the incident. Her legs felt weak and weakness washed over her whole body, the sickly aftermath of an adrenalin high.

Waveringly, she held out her arms to him. She badly needed some cuddling and comforting.

She must apologize to him and promise to heed his warnings in the future. He had been right and she should have listened.

His courage in standing his ground before the bear, gave her a new appreciation of his manliness. She felt humbled, humiliated by her own stupidity.

Kent's fear and relief had turned to anger.

"Where the hell is your gun?" he shouted. "Didn't I tell you never to leave the clearing without it?" He stood panting and glaring at her, the rush of adrenalin subsiding in him, too.

Still highly charged with emotion, he said, in a scornful voice trembling with emotion, "Your disobedience and stupidity nearly got us both killed."

Stunned, Annie let her arms drop. She knew that he was right, but this was not the way a man who loves you should talk after you have been terrified and nearly eaten. Especially after only three days of marriage.

Tears of rage and sorrow rolled from her eyes. "I was just bringing you your stupid damned lunch," she screamed, feeling hysteria rising again. "You unfeeling brute."

He made a motion to touch her, perhaps to take her into his arms.

"Don't touch me!" she shrieked, slapping at his hands. Sobbing, she stumbled blindly back along the path toward the cabin.

Kent followed to make sure she made it safely home.

As he walked along, he muttered "By the smell, that bear has been eating and rolling in salmon that spawned and died... died some time ago, to smell that strongly of rot. But, then, it has been about a month since the last run."

The cabin door slammed loudly behind her. Almost, he imagined, he could see the stout log structure shake. He stood, looking at the cabin.

Another loud bang echoed from within.

"Wow! I guess that I'd better let her alone for a while," he muttered. "That old bear was getting ready to go into hibernation – must have been a little short on stored up fat and looking for a dainty morsel. I'll have to keep my eyes open. Might have to shoot him yet, if he doesn't settle down."

Hungry, he turned and retraced his steps to where the hamper and bag lay abandoned by the path. Gathering them up, he took them to the bridge and sat down there to eat.

His mouth watered as he spread out the lunch. He said, "Aw, now, even fresh cookies. This is far better fare than I'm used to. Now I really feel like a creep."

His feeling of guilt grew as he ate.

"I really shouldn't have hollered at her like that," he said.

He hung his head and tried to excuse himself, "I just was so shaken up by the threat to her." Still, he knew that he had been in the wrong. He should have comforted her...time enough to make sure she understood the lesson, later.

Knowing he dared not go back to the cabin yet, he buried himself in hard work, punishing himself brutally as he pushed his muscles to capacity.

Hours passed, as he split and stacked wood until he was staggering. At last, he wiped the sweat from his brow and sat to rest.

"Stupid," he berated himself. "What I said to her was just so stupid."

Protesting muscles in both arms cramped painfully, causing the arms to curl involuntarily. He concentrated on relaxing them and, as the cramp eased, he massaged them back to life.

Kent gazed into the sky, his attention caught by the sudden lessening of light. A gust of chill wind made him shiver and he saw that the sky was rapidly clouding over.

A flurry of golden, falling leaves blew by, then another, and a sense of gloom settled over the land. Within the clouds, the sun was lowering toward the western peaks and dusk began to spread.

Hastily, he gathered up his saw and tools and fastened them to the back of the three wheeler.

Then, he climbed aboard his three wheeler and began the ride back to the cabin. As he went, large, fluffy, wet flakes of snow drifted from the sky, scattered at first, then growing thicker.

By the time Kent reached the clearing, the sun had set. Through the deepening dusk, he could see that nearly an inch of snow already blanketed the ground. It continued to sift from the sky.

He was alarmed to find that the cabin and clearing were dark and silent. Where was Annie?

He crossed the clearing and entered the cabin. It was cold. Going to the stove, he opened it and found that the fire was out. He concluded that it had been out for some time, because the ashes were cold.

"Annie?" he called. He listened hopefully for a reply.

There was no answer. Really worried now, he walked back to the bedrooms and opened the door to Annie's room. In spite of the darkness, he made out a huddled form on the bed. Relief washed through him. She had cried herself to sleep.

The need to talk this out with Annie rode him hard. First, though, he had better get the fire going... and the lights.

It was going to be a cold one tonight. Already, the thermometer outside the door read twelve below zero, and it felt like it was dropping fast.

The barometer bounded sharply downward in response to his tap. It was going to be a major fall storm for sure.

He built a fire in the stove, then went to start the generator and fetch in another armload of wood.

By the time he returned, the cabin was growing warmer and the main room was bright with yellow lamp light. Outside, the snow continued to drift down.

Without turning on the lights, he sat on the bed and reached out to touch her. "Annie?" he said, softly.

His hand met nothing but a heap of quilt. Annie was not there. The thrown back layers of quilts had fooled his eyes in the darkness. A lost feeling grew in the pit of his stomach.

From the other room came the sound of the grandfather clock striking. Automatically, he counted the strokes. Nine O'clock.

He loved that clock. It had become a habit, telling time by counting strokes. Especially useful here, in Alaska, where it was either dark all the time, or light all the time – you couldn't tell whether it was time to get up by looking at the light filtering in around the curtains.

Desperately, Kent searched... the other bedroom, the loft, the bathroom, the shop. No Annie. She was nowhere to be found.

The snow machine still crouched at the back of the shop, she couldn't have left. Surely, she wouldn't have walked.

Numbly, he wondered what to do next.

Arrived back at the cabin from his search of the shop, he spread his hands to the heat of the stove, warming them. He glanced about the room until a sheet of paper, propped up on the table, caught his eye. It must be a note from her.

He sprang to the table and snatched up the paper with shaking hands. It read *"I am sorry Kent. It is time for me to leave. I could tell by the way you spoke that you don't love me or want me and I am just a burden to you. We both just made a mistake, and it is time for me to correct it. Don't try to follow me or stop me. Annie."*

There was the stain of tear drops on the paper.

A great painful lump grew in Kent's throat. He groaned, "Oh Annie, I do love you and want you. We just need time. Damn it, I'm so sorry I yelled at you."

Tears stung his eyes. "Now she's out there struggling through the dark forest in the cold and snow because of my temper."

He hung his head, ashamed.

After a few moments he straightened. Grim resolve settled over his features. He must find her and bring her back, before this country killed her. This was no night for anyone to be out, let alone a cheechako. She must have headed for the road, for Maggie, or for town, he thought.

He gathered extra warm clothes and a sleeping bag to bundle her up in, once he found her.

A few moments pause sufficed to stuff the stove full of wood, and damp the fire, so that it would last. Then he strode out the door, into the snowy night.

The roar of the snow machine engine filled the unhearing night, then was quickly muffled by the heavy falling snow, as Kent rode off down the trail, into the surrounding wilderness.

He watched the trail carefully, and off to both sides. There was no sign of her tracks in the snow. That worried him, but what other way could she have gone?

She must have started out before the snow storm came.

“Dear God,” he prayed, “don’t let her be lost... please, don’t let her be lost.”

Kent knew that in any direction off the trail lay fifty to a hundred miles of rugged, trackless wilderness. There were no cabins except Blaine’s and, past his another nine miles or so, those along the highway and river.

There was only one right direction. He could only pray that she had taken it, and wouldn’t lose the trail in this storm.

The snow machine made quick work of the miles. Kent rode tensely, alert for any sign of her small form, hoping against hope that she would soon turn up unharmed.

The feeble beam of the headlight lit the fringe of timber and brush along the trail. But, beyond that, it was swallowed by the vast, cavernous, darkness, doubly dark for the snow clouds that blotted out the stars and moon.

He stroked the scar across his cheek.

Close spaced trunks of spruce and cottonwood, thick underbrush filling the gaps between them. It reminded him... of something... What? In the darkness, they began to close in on him, to change, taking a nightmare form out of the dark depths of his soul.

Another forest, another girl, sweet, warm, brown and giving... another time... "Juanita? Where are you? I came, where you said."

Bright orange tracer fire streaked the night, a string of explosions hammered his ears, curses, screams of agony and the wheezing, slobbering sobs of someone shot through the lungs – burned into his mind – a betrayal he could never forget. Stuttering machine guns, streaks of orange fire burned, again, across the darkness... jungle rain wet his face, or was it tears, or blood? Heavy impacts, the burning pain, his shoulder, his leg... the machette slash across his face burned anew.

Some inner strength aided him in forcing the nightmare away. Juanita was beyond his reach, beyond his help, it was Annie who needed him now. He mustn't fail her.

The orange tracer fire faded from his mind and, grimly, he steeled himself to search on. Yet there was no sign of her passing this way. He rubbed absent mindedly at the scar across his cheek. It throbbed and burned.

He was learning a hard lesson and he vowed that never again would he be harsh with her. He hadn't understood how proud and sensitive she was. She needed patient gentling, like a spirited filly.

A harsh sob was torn from Kent's throat, as the yellow lights of Blaine's cabin filtered through the falling snow. And he still had found no sign of her.

Blaine and Maggie would scorn him – he knew – but, at least, they would help him find her.

He pulled up before the cabin and stopped, shutting off the engine.

Earlier that day, when Annie had run across the clearing and into the cabin, she could see him following her. He had better stay away from her, the brute.

She threw the door shut behind her with a soul satisfying bang. Damn him! Damn him!

Her bedroom door, too, crashed shut behind her, as she threw herself down on the bed. There she lay, gulping and sobbing until the waves of fear and anger began to recede.

Kent was an insensitive, unfeeling brute, she thought hysterically. Just when she most needed his love and support, he had turned on her.

Too bad she couldn't talk to Maggie... tell her about it. Maggie would know what to do. But Maggie was at Blaine's, five miles away through the bush. Annie was thoroughly trapped. And she had done it to herself. How could she have been so stupid as to get herself into this mess? Damn! Damn! She had just let herself fall into it, like some spineless little ninny.

Angrily, she damned herself. All along she had let herself depend on someone else for everything, all the hard decisions. First Daddy. Then Clyde... thank the fates she hadn't married him. She had gained an inkling from Kent of the feeling a man could stir in a woman, and knew that marrying Clyde would have cheated them both. Vaguely, she hoped Clyde would find someone to love him.

Then she set out on her bold adventure to the city. Ha! Immediately, she had leeched onto Maggie, experienced "big sister" Maggie, and depended on her to take the lead, even into marriage and to Alaska.

And now she wanted only to depend on Kent for everything. Well! It was about time she developed a spine and learned to depend on herself. She could. She knew she could.

Worn out by the stressful events of the day, Annie dropped off to sleep. She slept heavily, as though drugged. As she slept and dreamed, her unconscious mind worked and a decision was formed.

When Annie woke, she was in the grip of a curious cold numbness. Too much emotion over the last week had overloaded her capacity for feeling.

The numbness was a symptom of shock, had she known, caused by the hysteria of the bear incident.

She knew, with a certitude formed while she slept, that she must leave. She had made a terrible mistake, for it was obvious that Kent didn't love her or want her.

If he did, she thought wildly, he would have sensed when she was ready and made love to her. And he never would have been so harsh and cruel after the horrifying experience with the bear.

He had wakened her sexual feelings, then cruelly frustrated them. She felt rejected and inadequate. This marriage was nothing like what she had hoped and dreamed.

She would escape and rebuild her life. Perhaps she could find some sort of job in Fairbanks, for now. Then, after she had saved a little money, she could go on to Hawaii. Yes, she could fall back on her other plan.

What time was it? She glanced at her watch. Nearly three O'clock. He would be back in another hour or two. It was time to go... quickly, if she was going to make good her escape.

As she hastily dressed in warm clothing, she considered. "He has the three wheeler. I guess that I have no choice but to walk. It's only five miles to the truck and he left the keys in it. I should be able to make that by eight or so, if I don't run into any trouble.

Tears ran down her cheeks, as she wrote him a note to be left on the table. She had dreamed such wonderful dreams – fantastic dreams – foolish dreams. She cursed herself for an idiot. No wonder he didn't want a clinging little ninny like her.

Well she would do just fine. They'd see.

Resolutely, she dressed herself for a journey, pulled on the warm boots he had given her, and the marten hat. She felt a pang of guilt. That had been a thoughtful gift.

"I can't face Maggie right now," she murmured, "I'm shamed. Besides, I won't jeopardize her happiness by involving her and her husband in my escape."

Annie pulled on the warm coat and put matches in an inner pocket. Moving to the bedroom, she took the wallet from her purse. She counted her money, hoping that, by some miracle, it had multiplied. It hadn't, of course.

"One hundred fifty four dollars and fourteen cents. That will hardly last any time at all. I had better get a job soon, doing what, I don't know. I'm sure there are no assembly lines here, but I'll find something."

With a regretful glance at her suitcases and clothes, she said, "I had better travel light through the forest. Maybe I can get these back, somehow, later on."

She stuffed her pockets with chocolate chip cookies on her way through the main room.

About to leave, her gaze fell upon the shotgun where it hung on the wall. She took the shotgun from its rack and a few extra shells. She had learned that lesson well. No wandering through the forest without a gun.

Annie went on out the door, shutting it quietly, but firmly behind her.

She crossed the clearing, without looking back, and entered the trail she had traveled on her wedding night. Was it only three days ago? It seemed ages. Such a short time for the slaying of her hopes and dreams.

The forest closed in around her, filtering out the sun with its thick branches. In the semi-darkness, it stirred with life. Here a squirrel, there a jay. Chickadees fluttered amongst the underbrush.

A ways further, a red fox stopped for a moment in the trail, peering intently at her with its intelligent eyes, the sharpness of his muzzle pointing at her. Then he leapt lightly off the trail and disappeared.

Once, her heart leaped into her throat at the sound of a heavy crashing in the brush, followed by a glimpse of a large black form.

A bear! Prickling chills ran up her spine, as she frantically checked the loads in the shot gun. She raised the gun into a ready position and peered apprehensively through the thicket.

The brush shook and crackled. The black form moved a little further, menacing, closer. Suddenly, she could see it clearly and her fear washed away on a tide of relief, as the big floppy ears and mule like nose of a cow moose appeared from the brush.

Gusts of hysterical giggles, left her leaning weakly against the trunk of a massive old cottonwood. With an effort, she pulled herself back together, and traveled onward.

Not much farther along the way, she rounded a bend and found water glittering before her. She gasped with dismay. How could she have forgotten the creek crossing? It rushed, gurgling and swirling, down the hill side, looking frighteningly swift and deep.

It would not be good to get wet feet, at this temperature, but how would she get across? There was no dry route visible... no log across the creek, and no stepping stones. Of course! Kent always rode across on the three wheeler. That didn't help her now.

Annie sighed and sat resignedly on a log. There she removed her boots, socks, pants and long john bottoms and made a neat bundle of them. Carrying the bundle and the shotgun high, she stood and stepped to the creek, her pearly bottom and legs glowing in the diffused light.

She trilled wild laughter, exclaiming, "I am glad no one can see me right now! Mrs. Schmidt would have a field day gossiping about this."

Had he been there, Kent would have found the sight stimulating. Her fine full curves were softly rounded, feminine, delicious.

A stifled shriek burst from her as she began to cross the creek. The water was just as she remembered it, like ice, and the stones bruised the soles of her delicate feet painfully. She had to plant her bare feet firmly to keep her footing on the slippery, wet rocks. With an iron determination, she forged onward across the wide, but fairly shallow, creek. It never did rise above knee deep.

Having arrived on the far side, she dried her feet and legs with handfuls of soft dry moss she found growing in a sheltered hollow beneath some spruce trees.

Then she dressed quickly, shivering, and sat on a cushion of the moss, leaning against the trunk of a spruce to rest. Her hysteria had faded to be replaced by a grim determination and a sense of pride in herself.

"I'm hungry," she said, surprised by a sudden pang in her middle. "No wonder, though, this has been a pretty strenuous work out and I didn't get any lunch." Regretfully, she pictured the crisp, golden fried chicken, elegant creamy potato salad, and deviled eggs, bright with sprinkles of red paprika. Saliva gushed into her mouth and her stomach rumbled.

"I hope that creep enjoyed my lunch," she muttered, resentfully. "Oh, well, at least, I've got some of the dessert."

She munched a few cookies, then rose to continue her journey on toward town.

To her surprise, the forest grew quiet as she went. She was unaware that the wild animals, just like her father's cows, seek shelter before a storm. The eerie silence seemed to have threatening quality.

The gloom deepened, as clouds covered the sky, and she felt a distinct chill. Soon, large, wet flakes of snow began to drift from the sky. The flakes were scattered, at first, then fell thicker, and thicker, until visibility was limited to fifty feet, or so, ahead of her. To make it worse, the sun was setting. In the growing dark, she wished that she had had the sense to grab a flash light.

A shiver ran up her spine. She began to feel doubtful. Did she really have what it takes?

"I've come much farther than seems right," she muttered. "Of course, walking instead of riding makes it seem different. I'm sure that I'm still on the trail, but I don't know if I can stay on the trail, if it gets dark before I get to Maggie's."

She was definitely on a trail, anyway, she reflected, and she had seen no others branching off. But had she missed one? What if she was headed over the ridge into Canada? She would die out here, before she ever made it that far.

Doggedly she pressed on, putting aside her worries.

As she proceeded, the snow was beginning to stick on the ground, a thin frosting of white. Please, Lord, don't hide the trail from me. It was growing dark. The prospect of having to spend the night, out here in the cold forest and snow, was decidedly unappealing. She was not dressed for it and had no sleeping bag or blankets.

She began to feel stirrings of fear. At another time, and under different circumstances, she would have thrilled to the beauty of the fresh, falling snow. Now, she felt threatened, depressed.

Around another bend in the trail, through the thickening gloom, a clearing opened up. Yellow light streamed from the windows of Blaine and Maggie's cabin, lighting the snow that continued to drift from the sullen, dark skies. Her heart bounded with a surge of relief, almost joy

– she had made it, after all.

And just over there, to her right, was Kent's pickup truck. He had, she remembered, left his keys hanging in the ignition.

A glance at her watch showed that it was seven forty-two. She had made good time, but she had better hurry on. He would be coming after her any time. But maybe he wouldn't. Why should he? She had been pretty definite in her note.

Annie moved stealthily along the edge of the clearing, careful to keep out of the golden path of light that spilled from the windows and across the snow. Reaching the truck, she exhaled the breath that she had unconsciously been holding, and climbed in.

She shut the door quietly and sat a moment, resting her forehead on the steering wheel. She was tired, so tired. Maybe she should just rest a while.

No! She couldn't stop now, she thought, and jerked erect, listening. "Good, the generator is running loud enough that I doubt they'll hear the truck when I start it. If they do, I will just have to make a run for it."

She pumped the gas, and turned the key. The starter seemed unnaturally loud. "Please, please... start," she whispered, as it ground over and over. Then the engine coughed, sputtered, and purred to life. She turned on the windshield wipers to clear the snow from the windshield.

There was no sign of alarm from the cabin, yet. Her stomach rolled uneasily with tension. She controlled it fiercely. There was no time, right now, for stopping to vomit.

The headlights would have to stay off until she was across the creek and down the road a ways. She would have to gamble that there was enough light to get that far safely.

Easing the truck into gear, she gave it a little gas, increasing the pressure on the gas peddle slowly, to avoid alerting them in the cabin with sudden roar of the engine, then eased out the clutch.

The truck rolled across the yard, picking up speed, and splashed across the creek.

In the rear view mirror, the cabin appeared tranquil, still. She let several bends in the road fall behind her and the cabin lights disappear, before switching on the truck's head lights.

A wave of relief washed over her, she had made it this far. Her nervous stomach settled and now she felt nothing but tiredness.

Later the sadness would come, she knew, but just now she was only tired.

It came as a surprise when the road met the highway, suddenly emerging from the brush and trees. She turned onto it and drove toward Fairbanks. The driving was tensely demanding, for the accumulating snow made the highway slippery and treacherous.

She drove slowly, her neck and shoulder muscles tight with the tension. The steady swish swish of the wipers was hypnotic, and the miles went by.

After a long drive through the darkness, the lights of the town were a welcome sight, appearing first as a glow on the horizon, then growing to a blaze of white that reflected from the underside of the clouds. Annie pulled into the first gas station she came to and rolled down her window.

An older man, grey haired and kindly looking, came out.

Too old to be working as an attendant, she thought. She supposed he must be the owner.

"Can you tell me where's the cheapest place to stay a night?" Annie called out, "...and how to get there?"

The old man studied her with his sharp eyes, seeing the signs of stress and fatigue on her face.

He directed her to a place that charged thirty-five dollars a night. Rates in Alaska were evidently much higher than at home.

"It isn't much, but it's clean and warm," he said.

He hesitated a moment, then said, in a fatherly manner, "Down on your luck?"

Reluctantly, but drawn by his manner, she nodded.

"Yes," she said. "I've only enough money to last for three or four days. I need to find a job."

He said, "Ma – my wife, that is – runs a cafe here in town... Just a minute." He walked into the station office and returned, to hand her a card.

"There's the address. I know she's looking for a new waitress, doesn't mind training," he said.

He glanced at his wrist, then shook his head, saying, "She's off now. But go see her around noon tomorrow."

"She works the noon to nine shift herself," he explained. "Closes at nine."

Annie looked at the card, then put it in a pocket. "I'll go see her," she said. "I don't know how I can thank you Mr..." She paused.

"Simmons," he supplied. His face wrinkled with a broad grin. It shone in his eyes. Then he added, "Just call me Pops. I'll tell her you are coming."

She smiled, tremulously, and said, "Ok, Pops. Thank you." She put the truck in gear and drove off.

Pops watched her go, wondering what her story was. Well, Ma would be glad to hire her. She always had more help than she needed, poor girls who needed a break.

On the way to the hotel, Annie stopped at a grocery store. Shopping carefully for the cheapest prices, she got cold cuts, pop, cheese and bread, toothbrush and paste, a comb and lipstick.

Tomorrow, before she got rid of the truck, she would have to get an inexpensive skirt, blouse and flat shoes.

She drove on down the street, having no trouble finding the place. Pops gave good clear directions. Unfortunately, the hotel Pops had directed her to had no vacancies, unusual in the winter... but there were sled dog races going on this week, all the indian villagers had come for them from their homes in the bush. But they recommended another nearby.

She parked the truck, carefully concealing it behind the dumpster out back... just in case they were already looking for her.

The hotel had little to recommend it, other than being clean and warm, but that was enough for the moment. It was vastly better than a bed of moss under a spruce tree.

After a sandwich and can of pop, she visited the bathroom, down the hall, then settled into the covers, ready for the night.

Come morning she would look for a job. In the likely event that nothing better showed up, she would go see Ma at noon.

Aches and pains assaulted her in her poor bruised feet and the calves of her legs. Most of all, she became aware of an aching hurt deep in her heart. Kent's handsome face floated in her mind, an expression of hurt and concern on it.

Tears trickled down her cheeks, soaking into the pillow.

CHAPTER NINE

Kent got off his snow machine and stood up, just as the cabin door burst open, spilling light in a long rectangle across the snow.

Blaine and Maggie appeared in the doorway, framed in the golden light. Maggie had a soft, sated look on her face, and a slow sexy sleepy look about her eyes. Her red curls were tousled.

Both Blaine and Maggie were bare foot and wore a robe over, it looked like, nothing else.

Oh, oh, thought Kent. I obviously have interrupted something. I reckon that I'm probably just about as welcome as a skunk at a house warming party. Less so, when they hear my news. – On occasion he still used expressions his parents had carried from the Ozarks, when they moved on to Arizona.

"Hi, Kent," Blaine said. He sounded surprised – they hadn't planned any get togethers during the first weeks of their honeymoons. He waited in silence, obviously expecting Kent to say something, to explain his presence.

Maggie looked at him questioningly, too, and finally asked, "Where's Annie?"

He felt his face contort, in an expression of pure misery. Choking back a sob, he said, gravely, "I had hoped that you would know."

He bowed his head and stood in silence.

Heedless of her bare feet and the snow, Maggie ran to him. She put her hands on his arm in impulsive sympathy and tugged at him gently.

"Come in, Kent," she urged. "Tell us about it."

He saw soft compassion in her blue eyes, as he gazed into them in the spill of light. With a nod, he let her lead him inside. There, she sat him down in a chair by the wood stove.

Blaine opened the stove's damper wide, threw in a handful of dry, finely split wood, and the fire began to huff, sounding rather like a steam engine.

The waves of heat felt good. He hadn't realized how chilled he was.

Blaine and Maggie sat facing him on the couch, where Blaine took her delicate, high arched feet in his hands, massaging the cold out of them.

The silence dragged on until, at length, Blaine cleared his throat. "Well now, what's wrong, partner?" he asked.

Kent felt shame faced, felt his ears burning red. "Annie has run away from me but she doesn't know this country. I'm afraid that she may be lost, out in this storm. She may freeze if I can't find her and I haven't been able to find any trace of her trail."

After moments of stunned silence, Maggie gasped, "Oh, Kent, what went wrong?... I know she was worried about the first night. Did you hurt her?... or shame her?"

Her voice had started out soft and concerned, but grew harder with a demanding note as she continued.

Kent saw the flare of rising celtic temper in her reddening face and flashing eyes. Obviously Maggie was leaping to a conclusion, and concluding the worst.

Blaine leapt up, hastily. He said, "Maggie, now is not the time for recriminations. If poor Annie is lost out there... she may die, if we don't get out there and find her. We need to do it soon, too."

There was a curious stiffness to Blaine's expression. Kent was certain that Blaine, too, thought the worst of him.

Kent's heart ached but he stifled the urge to explain. It would take too long. What Blaine said was true. Right now, time was of the essence. They must find Annie, before it was too late.

He said, "Please get dressed and help me find her, I'll explain later, I promise."

Blaine had already vanished into the bedroom. Maggie lingered a moment, her blue eyes studying his face intently. Reading something in his eyes, she said, in a low voice, almost a husky growl, "If you have hurt her, I'll slash your balls off."

She didn't wait for a reply, but turned and left, going into the bedroom to dress for the storm. There was no doubt in his mind that she was in deadly earnest, like a mother tiger guarding her cub.

Kent held his hands to the fire and struggled to collect his thoughts. He raised his bowed head as Blaine returned, still buttoning his shirt.

"We have got to have a plan," Blaine said. "What made you think that she came here?"

Kent dug the note out of his pocket and handed it over to Blaine.

He said, "She left this note. It sounds to me like she planned to go to town, and this is the only way she could have come... unless she got lost."

Maggie had just come back into the room. She leaned against Blaine and read the note aloud. "I am sorry, Kent. It is time for me to leave. I could tell by the way you spoke that you don't love me or want me and I am just a burden to you. We both just made a mistake – and it is time for me to correct it. Don't try to follow me or stop me. Annie."

Maggie glared at him "I noticed the tear stains on the note," she said, meaningfully.

Blaine broke in. "That almost sounds like a suicide note to me," he said.

Maggie exclaimed, "Oh, no!" Tears gushed from her eyes and she hid her face in her hands.

"Oh God," Kent groaned, "I wish that you hadn't said that. It does sound that way and now I feel like my guts were just ripped out."

"Wait!" Blaine yelled, holding his hands up in a halting gesture. "I'm sorry I mentioned it, it contributes nothing. Let's consider the most likely possibilities."

There was a moment of silence as they thought. Maggie saw an odd expression grow on Kent's face.

Suddenly, Kent whirled and burst out through the door. He ran across the yard to where the pickups were parked.

His whoops of joy dragged Blaine and Maggie out to stand beside him, looking at the spot where his truck was, inarguably, not parked. The wheel tracks in the snow led out, across the creek, and disappeared in the darkness... down the road, toward town. They were fresh, made within the hour.

"What a relief," Blaine said. "At least, we know that she's not lost out in the woods."

"Yes," Kent said, "and that she hasn't committed suicide." He looked sharply at Blaine.

Blaine caught the look. "I'm sorry, partner," he apologized, "I could have bit off my tongue, as soon as I said that. But, of course, it was too late then. We were grasping at straws."

The tracks were half snowed over by the soft flakes that continued to drift from the sky. But that didn't matter, there was only one place for them to go.

"Lend me your truck," Kent demanded. He was impatient to be after her.

"Now that we know she is ok, don't you think you should wait until morning?" asked Blaine. "It's nearly ten o'clock and pitch dark."

Kent rejected that, saying, "No! What if she's headed for the airport?" He was frantic at the thought of losing her permanently.

Maggie said, "She doesn't have the money for that. I know she has only about a hundred and fifty dollars."

Kent relaxed marginally. "Plane fare is five hundred or more even just to Seattle – and over two hundred to Anchorage," he said, "So she's trapped in Fairbanks."

He thought a minute, then shook his head. He said, "I still have to go after her now. What if she went off the road in this? She might still die. There won't be much traffic, if any, on a night like this."

"You do have that packet of food and survival gear in the back of the truck," Blaine reminded him.

"Yes," Kent said. "But it's in a garbage bag. She would never find it, because she would probably just think that it *is* a bag of garbage."

Blaine came to a decision.

"We'll come with you," he said. He opened the driver's door and slid beneath the steering wheel. As Maggie and Kent came around the other side and slid in, he started the engine.

They bounced, splashing, across the creek and headed down the road toward the highway.

The back end of the truck displayed an alarming tendency to fish tail on the curves, because of the accumulating snow.

If they ran off the road on this stretch, Blaine thought, they would be there all night, while one of them made the long walk back to the cabin for the snow machine and a winch. He cursed himself for not thinking to bring the twelve volt winch with them. It never paid to be in a hurry. In this country it could be fatal.

"Kent," Maggie said, pinning him with an unwavering stare, "What did happen?" She said it firmly, obviously not intending to be put off any further.

There was an embarrassed silence.

"Did you hurt her the first night, Kent?" she pressed.

Kent's face reddened. This was hard for him, but obviously she felt no mercy. And he couldn't blame her. Annie was her best friend, her only real friend... except Blaine, but that was different.

"There hasn't been a first night yet," Kent choked out, humiliated.

Maggie looked shocked, in the dim light from the dash board. "No wonder she thinks you don't want her," she said. Her freckles stood out on her face, which had reddened dangerously. And her eyes were sparkling with angry fire.

Kent argued, "But Maggie, she asked me, herself, to give her a little time, because she was frightened and didn't know me yet."

The red began to fade. Maggie looked faintly amused. She said, "Hmmm... and then she expected you to sense it when she was ready, and you did nothing about it... Didn't you know that husbands are expected to be mind readers?" She chuckled.

Kent laughed, ruefully, and said, "No, I didn't. And I'm afraid that I'm not."

Maggie looked thoughtful, then insisted, "There must have been more reason than that for her to run away." The look she turned on him was dubious, questioning. "Her note said you told her you didn't love her."

Blaine turned the truck onto the main highway, headed for Fairbanks, and increased speed. The snow was more beaten down here, though more continued to fall from the sky, and driving was a little easier.

Kent protested, "I told her no such thing."

He went on to explain, "I made sure she knew how to shoot the shotgun... told her never to leave the cabin without it, because of bears. Well, when she came to bring my lunch out to where I was cutting wood today, she didn't bring the gun."

Kent gulped, remembering his fear for her, and continued, "A grizzly bear attacked her, frightened her near to death. I got between her and the bear and drove it off but, then, I was so shook up that I cussed her out for being stupid and disobedient."

Maggie looked horrified. She said, "A bear! Blaine warned me of the danger, but I thought it was just a tale... I didn't really take it seriously. They are always portrayed as being so nice... you know, Gentle Ben, and all like that."

Blaine broke in. "It is serious... deadly serious," he said earnestly. "Bears are around here frequently and they can be very dangerous. The people who make those lying movies should be sent to prison."

"So she needed to be held and comforted, loved, reassured, and you cussed her out... called her stupid and disobedient," Maggie said, her tone severe.

Kent hung his head, "Yes," he said. "That's why she wrote, 'I could tell by the way you spoke that you don't love me or want me.' I meant to apologize later but she was gone when I got back to the cabin."

"Kent, we have to find her!" Maggie exclaimed. "I'm sure you can bring her back home if you apologize, then sweep her up in your arms and kiss her until she gains her senses... or loses them, as the case may be."

Maggie looked at Kent and smiled, adding, "And, Kent, when you get her home... take her into the bedroom. Be firm, be tender and be gentle, but make her do it. Consummate the marriage, make her fully your wife."

She laughed heartily, seeing Kent's face turn scarlet in the light from the dash.

They drove on through the blackness, snow flakes falling thickly in their headlight beams. The only sound was thc swish of the wipers and the hum of the tires.

A glow on the horizon foretold their approach to Fairbanks. Blaine asked, "What is our plan? Where would she go?"

"I suppose that her first thought would be to get a room for the night. It'd have to be a cheap one, she certainly couldn't afford these hundred dollar a night tourist hotels," said Maggie.

"Well, that should be easy to check... There aren't that many cheap hotels or bed and breakfasts in town," Blaine replied.

"Maybe we should ask if they've seen her at gas stations, too," Kent added.

"Well, here's the first one, coming up," Blaine said, as he turned off the road and pulled up to the pumps.

Their presence brought the owner hurrying out, wiping his hands off on a grease rag.

"Hi Pops," Blaine said. "Fill 'er up please. And, Pops? We're looking for a girl. A pretty girl. Amber hair like honey, big hazel eyes, mostly green, about five foot six tall. Have you seen her this evening?"

Pops hedged. "What makes you think the young lady wants to be found?" he asked. He started the gas running into the truck's tank.

"She's Kent's new wife. She ran off, Pops," Blaine confided.

"Well, now, a young wife must have a pretty good reason for running off," Pops said gruffly.

Blaine sensed that Pops knew something. "Come on Pops," he drawled. "It was a lover's quarrel. You know what I mean." He used his confidential 'man to man' tone of voice.

A twinkle came to Pops eyes. "Ah," he said. "I remember it well. When I first married Ma... well, that's a whole 'nother story."

A far away look had come into his eyes.

"Well?" Blaine prompted.

"Oh, yes. She stopped here earlier this evening, looking for a room and a job. I sent her to this place," he pointed to one of the ads above the pumps, "and told her to go see Ma at the cafe, about noon tomorrow."

The pump clicked off and he racked the nozzle. Blaine handed him a ten, saying, "Keep the change."

"Thanks, Pops. Thanks a lot," Kent added. He was feeling much better, now, hopeful again.

"Be good to her, Kent, she seems like a mighty sweet young girl," Pops said. There was a big grin on his face, as he watched them drive away.

Later, Kent sat in a chair in Blaine and Maggie's room. They had all just checked in.

Blaine poured him a glass of scotch from a bottle they had picked up on the way.

Kent raised it, tipped it up and swallowed. The big gulp of scotch burned all the way down. He toyed with the glass, turning it in his hands, holding it up to see the light shining amber through it. "Damn it," he said, "I was so sure that we would catch up with her tonight."

Maggie looked at him sympathetically. She said, "Kent, we might as well get some sleep. It's two in the morning. You can catch up with her at Ma's Cafe. And you'll function better for having had some rest."

Kent nodded. "I'll go on to my room, so you two can get to bed," he said. "Maybe I can even sleep a little."

He tossed off the rest of the scotch, shuddered, and left, carrying the bottle.

As he closed the door, he heard Maggie softly say, "Good night, Kent. Don't drink too much of that nerve medicine."

Annie hadn't been at the hotel. It was full and the clerk that had been on duty until eleven was off shift.

Kent's truck was no where to be found.

He drank another glass of scotch, more slowly. Once in bed, he tossed fitfully, but finally drifted off to sleep.

Scraps of conversation filtered through the door. Somewhere, a vacuum cleaner was running. Kent groaned and stirred, unused to noises when he slept. What was going on? Where was he?

Remembering, he jerked upright. His feet hit the floor and he sat erect on the edge of the bed, pulling himself together. He picked up his watch from the bed side table and saw that it was nearly ten o'clock. A faint throbbing in his forehead and an acid taste in his mouth reminded him of last night's scotch consumption.

Anxiety and anticipation stirred queasily in his belly.

He picked up the phone and rang Blaine and Maggie, to be sure they were up. Then he sprinted to the shower.

Concealed amongst other cars and trucks in a parking lot across the street, Kent watched the front of Ma's Cafe sharply.

He felt renewed by the shower and a good breakfast. But he was worried. Noon, and she was still not here. He fidgeted restlessly. What if she didn't show up? Could she have taken off driving to Anchorage? There was a sinking, sick feeling in his stomach. He looked at his companions.

Maggie and Blaine were watching silently. There was nothing to be said. Nothing to be done. Just wait... and hope.

A boy came out of the cafe and began to shovel the walk out front. Kent watched him, as the minutes ticked by. Nearly one, and still no Annie. She wasn't going to show up. He continued to watch, having no better option in mind. Women came and went, customers of the cafe. But none of them was Annie, not even close.

What would he do if she didn't show up here? He tried to think of other possibilities. Maybe he could file a missing persons report with the police. She had to be in town. Unless, oh *God*! Unless she had hitch hiked, or driven his truck south. The thought was like a blow in the belly. His lips moved in a silent prayer.

Suddenly, he saw her. "Down," he hissed, to Blaine and Maggie. "Don't let her see us." His mouth went dry. In his ears, he could hear the thunder of his heart. "Thank you, Lord," he breathed.

She was coming up the walk, looking about nervously. He crouched, peering over the top of the dash board, and his heart went out to her.

Annie looked timid and downcast. Her shoulders sagged. Her mouth drooped at the corners. She wore a cheap black skirt and white blouse. She must have bought them here in town especially for this interview.

Kent tensed as she approached the front of the cafe. Now! He sprang out of the truck and ran to her, sprinting like an Olympic runner, pushing himself for his maximum speed.

She saw him coming and turned to dart away, but he caught up to her and grabbed her roughly by the right arm. "Wait!" he ordered.

At his command, her eyes began to flash dangerously. Kent saw that she was about to speak.

Quickly, he forestalled her. "I've come to apologize," he said. His words tumbled out. "I love you and want you. And I have come to take you home."

Kent began to pull Annie into his arms, ignoring her frown and down turned mouth.

He heard a squeal of rage, just before her hard little right fist connected solidly with his right eye.

Staggering back, he raised his hand to feel his already discoloring eye. A groan rumbled deep from within him.

"Ohh!" Annie said. "Ohh, Kent!" She was overcome with regret. Her arms flew around his neck and she raised her lips to his.

Her instinctive gesture of warmth and tenderness stirred Kent's blood and he wrapped her tightly in his long arms, setting himself to kissing her thoroughly, forgetting his wounded eye entirely.

As his lips plundered hers, she melted against him, her blood stirred to what seemed near boiling.

He trailed kisses and nibbles down the side of her neck, so distracting her that she was helpless to resist, as he lifted her in his arms and carried her off toward the truck.

"What do you think you're doing?" she stammered.

"Taking you home," he said, and laughed. Just then, Blaine pulled the truck up beside him and Maggie opened the door.

Kent swung up easily, onto the passenger seat, and settled Annie in his lap. Her arms clung around his neck.

"You said you love me?" she questioned softly, oblivious to the others. A shy smile moved across her lips.

"Very much, darling," he reassured her. His eyes met hers and an electric charge flowed between them.

"Kent," she said. Her voice was breathy. Then she frowned.

"You were cruel yesterday," she accused softly. Her gaze became challenging.

Kent nodded. He said, "I'm sorry. I was right to be angry but, just then, I should have comforted you, not berated you. I'll never be harsh with you again."

He stroked her cheek, gently. She responded by snuggling her cheek into his palm.

She said, "Yes. That was wrong. I was terrified and humiliated. I needed to be comforted. Perhaps I still do." She said it so quietly, that he had to strain to hear her.

Taking the cue, Kent tightened his arms and drew her head onto his shoulder. With a long, shuddering sigh, she relaxed there. He buried his face in her hair.

"Kent?" she murmured.

"Yes?"

"I'm sorry too. I'll pay attention to what you tell me in the future," she said. "I know you're just trying to protect me. Then she felt her lip begin to quiver and tears sprang to her eyes.

She sobbed softly, "I was about to tell you that yesterday, when you started yelling at me."

Embarrassed by her crying, Annie gave a deprecating little laugh and said, "I'm sorry about the tears, I can't seem to stop."

She drew a deep breath. "I remember what Dad told me once: 'Marriage is like a waltz; two steps forward, two steps back. Yielding, not leading. Flowing together.' We have to remember that, too."

Tenderly, Kent took her mouth with his. Feeling her warm response, he nibbled her lower lip and kissed the corner of her mouth.

His lips slid up her cheeks... one then the other, kissing away the tears. The last of her sadness was swamped by the flow of blood to her lips and a growing warmth somewhere in her middle.

Kent held her tightly again, her head on his shoulder.

Softly she mumbled, "You were so brave – standing your ground against that big bear, defending me."

Maggie broke in. "Annie, where is Kent's truck?" she asked, "We can go pick it up."

Annie squirmed around to face her, not leaving the refuge of Kent's arms. Maggie looked unrepentant for her role in this kidnaping. Annie glared at her, her lower lip protruding.

"You all conspired against me," she accused, "Even you, my best friend."

"Never against you, Kid... For you! Always," Maggie said, with a smile. "We all love you. And we just wanted to get you back where you belong."

Mollified, Annie directed them to the place where she had hidden Kent's truck, behind the dumpster in the hotel's back parking lot. Kent carried her to it and slid her gently onto the seat.

"You go on ahead," Blaine called. "Maggie and I are going to stay over and do a night on the town. You might as well use our place tonight and put off the trip back to your place until tomorrow. You both need the rest."

Kent acknowledged that offer with a wave and drove off with Annie snuggled tight against him, her arms around his chest. The fingers of his right hand toyed with her hair, as her head lay against his chest.

"Never again, Annie," he promised, "Never again will I give you orders. From now on it's fifty-fifty, everything we do we'll discuss and agree on."

He was rewarded by a warm snuggling of her cheek against his chest and a tightening of her arms around him.

Outside the window, a wonderland stretched off into the distances. The snow had stopped and the sun shown, golden in the blue sky. It glistened from the pure, white snow that blanketed the land and frosted the trees and brush.

Along the way, lulled by the hum of the tires on the pavement, she dropped off to sleep, overcome by the lingering effect of her exertions and the emotional stress.

Kent drove slowly, heeding the drag of snow on his tires. Once off the main highway and headed down his road, the deep snow was treacherous and he had to resume driving with two hands on the wheel. The drive was difficult and tiring.

At last, the truck splashed across Blaine's creek, breaking a thin skim of ice, and came to rest in its own parking place.

Carefully, he gathered her into his arms, smiling as she snuggled in, secure and trusting, and carried her into Blaine's cabin. She didn't awaken. Poor little gal, she is exhausted, he thought, regretting his role in causing her ordeal. In the bed room, he deposited her gently on the bed and began to unbutton her blouse, thinking to make her more comfortable.

She protested sleepily, groaned, and mumbled, “Tired, so tired.”

Kent stopped trying to undress her and, instead, settled down beside her, and gathered her into his arms, pulling the quilt over both of them.

As he lay holding her, he was acutely aware of an aching tension in his groin. He loved her and it was nearly time to do something about making her fully his wife. But not tonight, she deserved her rest. She had suffered a hard experience these last two days.

At last, Kent, too, dropped off to sleep and they slept in each other’s arms until dawn.

CHAPTER TEN

Grey light, filtering through the curtains at the window, caught Kent's attention as he stirred and opened his eyes. Beside him, Annie slept on, a smile on her lips. Her arm was thrown across his chest.

With a groan, he eased out of bed, careful not to disturb her rest. He padded sock foot into the main room, shivered, and renewed the fire, to take off the morning chill. Next he fixed the coffee pot and set it on the stove to perk. Getting started in the morning was damned difficult, unless he had a good stout cup of coffee – he needed the high octane stuff too, none of this decaf. With an appreciative sniff, as the pot began to perk, he identified this as a good Colombian.

He remembered Maggie's advice. "Be firm, tender and gentle, but make her do it. Consummate the marriage, make her fully your wife."

Today would be the day he carried out a campaign of seduction. But first, he would start the electricity and take a shower. He felt grimy and uncomfortable after sleeping all night in his clothes. Then he would take her home, for he wanted it to happen at his home, not here.

Outside, the snow fell again, joining the three feet that had already accumulated on the ground. It was a beautiful winter day. A good day to start a honeymoon.

By the time Kent stepped from the shower, refreshed, and vigorously toweled himself dry, the coffee he had put on the stove was perked.

He helped himself to a cup, grunting with satisfaction as the first swallow spread warmth down his insides. He set down the cup and walked to the bedroom.

Annie stretched sensuously and smiled, in response to his gentle kiss. She had been conscious of his arms about her during the night. Why didn't he follow through and possess her? she wondered.

There was a tender expression on his face. Perhaps this was the moment. Excitement began to stir.

"I have the shower running, Annie," he said. "Sleeping in your clothes all night must have made you uncomfortable. Why don't you hop in. I'll have breakfast ready when you are through."

He brushed his lips gently over hers, leaving an expectant tingling, and gently nibbled the side of her neck.

His eye was purple and blue, she noted, nearly swollen closed. She kissed it softly. "Oh, your poor eye. I'm so sorry that I did that," she murmured.

"It's all right. I probably deserved that," he said. "Go ahead and take your shower, it'll feel good."

He straightened and turned to go. Disappointment was sour in her stomach as she watched him leave. It was her own fault. Why had she been such a reluctant little virgin? Sighing, she sat up and swung her feet to the floor.

She supposed that she would have to take the initiative.

Kent was right, she thought, as usual... damn him, it would probably be the pattern of her life. Her clothes had chafed and bound upon her during the night. And now the hot water, cascading down over her unfettered body, brought a luxurious feeling of well being.

She turned, letting the heat soak into her neck and shoulders.

Somehow, she would lure him into consummating the marriage before this day was over. A subtle pleasant tension grew as she made this vow.

"Kent?" she called enticingly, as she walked out of the shower room, wearing Maggie's filmy, peach colored peignoir.

She had belted the peignoir tight against her, so it would outline her figure.

He turned and she felt his eyes stripping the garment from her. He wore a barbecue apron over his denim trousers and shirt, and was busy at the cook stove. Several skillets steamed there, putting out inviting aromas that reminded her how hungry she was. But she was hungry for something else, too.

"Yes, Sweetheart?" he said.

The pet name roused a feeling of tenderness. Perhaps she should just throw off the peignoir. That should be a direct enough invitation, even for him!

She saw his sharp eyes take note of the crimson tide rising from her neck and up across her face.

No, she couldn't be that brazen. Somehow she had to get him to take the initiative. She gulped, losing heart. "What are your plans for the day?" she asked meekly.

A lazy smile crossed his lips. His eyes stroked the calves of her legs.

"Sweetheart, we are going to take the day off and honeymoon," he drawled, "And tomorrow too."

Her stomach lurched with a sudden feeling of expectancy. Was there a twinge of fear? Yes. She firmly suppressed it.

He continued, "First I'm going to feed you a breakfast of Spanish Omelette, link sausage and fried potatoes... to keep your strength up."

His face wore an impish expression that left no doubt in her mind about what she would need her strength for.

"Then," he said, "I want to take you for a snow machine ride. I'm going to take you on the longer trail home, up on the ridge, so that you can see out over this marvelous piece of country..."

Annie broke in. "A snow machine ride?" she said excitedly. That was one of the things she had looked forward to.

"Sure thing, that's how I got here yesterday," Kent replied. "Come, look out." He crossed to the front door, opened it, and pointed out.

Annie crossed the floor and stood looking out at the winter wonderland.

His snow machine crouched, just outside the door, covered in snow. The air was a little chilly but pleasant and fresh.

Lost in the beauty, she was hardly aware of him coming up behind her until his arms slid around her, his hands clasping the swelling curve of her hips.

She nestled back against his muscular frame. "And after the snow machine ride?" she breathed.

He nibbled her right ear lobe, then whispered, huskily, "I thought perhaps we could fish off the bridge on the way down from the ridge, to catch supper, if you like. Fresh caught Arctic Grayling is a real treat."

"That sounds like fun," she agreed. "And then what?"

"After I bring you home and fill you with hot chocolate and brandy... then, well, why don't we play that by ear?" he said.

His hands traveled up the front of her body. She moaned, and arched her back, as he cupped her breasts through the peignoir.

A kitchen timer buzzed annoyingly. He kissed her neck.

"Oh oh," he exclaimed. "I'd better pay attention to breakfast, unless you want a burnt offering." He released her, and went to the stove.

Annie looked out the door a moment longer. The tension was unbearable, almost an agony. Why didn't he just do it to her? Couldn't he tell that she was ready?

She closed the door, turned, and gave him her prettiest smile. "Well, I guess that I'll get dressed then," she said as she crossed to the bedroom. She removed the peignor reluctantly.

Even more reluctantly, she began to dress. Her first garment was her long johns, feminine ones, with a dainty floral print... pink roses. She had bought these when she was still on the farm.

It had never snowed there, the way it did here, so deep and fluffy. Certainly, never in September. And in the city, well, there, even the snow had been dirty and grey.

Eager with anticipation, she pulled on the socks and jeans she had worn yesterday and her sweatshirt.

Her shoulder length hair, she combed out straight, and it curled in a soft wave on either side of her face.

She studied herself in the mirror, noting a slightly fevered brightness in her eye and pink flush in her cheeks. She nodded approvingly.

"Just in time," Kent said, as she walked into the main room. "Everything is ready." He let his eyes study her intently.

"Especially me," she thought.

After a long, low whistle, he exclaimed, "You are gorgeous, Sweetheart."

Finally feeling like a bride, Annie crossed to sit at the table. It had taken a little time, but Kent didn't feel like a stranger to her now.

Breakfast was delicious and Kent waited on her attentively. He made her feel treasured.

When, at last, she put down her fork, she was stuffed.

She said, "If I had known you were such a good cook, I would have proposed to you long ago."

Kent chuckled. He said, "I wish that I had known long ago that you were available. We've wasted a lot of time... Coffee?" He held the pot over her mug, inquiringly.

She nodded. "Yes, it will give breakfast a few minutes to settle, before we go."

Kent poured, and handed her the steaming mug, then crossed the room to return with mukluks and hats. He put them down in easy reach, and rained a trail of nibbling kisses down the side of her neck.

Annie arched her neck, to make it easier for him. Her sense of urgent want grew stronger, and she moaned when he left off kissing her and returned to his chair.

If he wasn't careful, she was going to attack him before the day was over, despite her shyness.

They drank the coffee, then Kent cleared the table. Together, they made quick work of the dishes. He sang to her as they worked. Though she never had been a singer before, she found herself joining him in a duet... dishwater dripping from her hands.

The dishes done, he sat at the table and pulled on his mukluks. She followed suit. Then, they put on coats and hats and she followed him outdoors to the snow machine.

He swept the snow off it with his gloved hands. It crouched there, long and black, a little daunting in its unfamiliarity.

He put her shotgun in a sheath riveted to the cowling.

Climbing aboard, He patted the long seat and said, "Sit here behind me and put your arms around my waist."

She climbed aboard and wrapped her arms around him. In response to a turn of the key, the engine sputtered to life.

Kent backed the snow machine around and shifted gears to head it toward the path leading up the valley.

Annie hugged him tightly around his waist, intensely aware of his hard rippling torso muscles and the heady, disturbing musk scent of the shaving lotion he had splashed on.

The morning's fall of snow had been short-lived and it was another clear golden day.

Plumes of steam from their breath blew back, mingling in the crisp air with blowing snow thrown up by the wind of their passage. Trees whipped by, with an exhilarating rush, as they sped higher, taking a branching trail angling up the side of the long, snow covered ridge.

She felt so full of life, so different than she had ever felt in the city. Her face and hands stung in the cold, yet her blood surged, singing through her veins.

Suddenly, she flinched and squealed as birds exploded from the snow seemingly right under them.White birds seemed to be everywhere, scattering in all directions in a thundering uproar of drumming wing beats.

Kent eased to a stop and turned off the engine. They watched the birds settling to the snow in scattered groups. They were calling to each other in voices that were, comically, rather like Woody

Woodpecker's.

"Ptarmigan," he said, "Sort of like grouse and pretty good to eat."... He laughed. "There is a town, over across those mountains," he pointed, "that they wanted to name Ptarmigan. But no one could spell it, so they named it Chicken instead."

Then he asked, "Are you doing all right?"

She hugged him more tightly, resting her head dreamily against his back and nodding. She could go on like this forever, it seemed to her.

"We're nearly to the top," he said. He restarted the machine and drove it on up the slope, until they came out on top of the ridge. There he stopped.

Several folded ranges of low mountains rolled off to the south and east below them. Further off a mightier, jagged range of mountains clawed their way into the sky, bluish from distance. The far end faded gradually into the western horizon.

Annie caught her breath and gasped, "Oh, Kent, they are beautiful." She had lived all her life in flat prairie country. And the city was located there too, so she had never known the majesty of the mountains.

"That's the Alaska Range," he told her. "And look down there." He stretched out his arm and pointed.

She followed his pointing finger with her eyes. "Why there's our cabin," she said. "It looks like a toy from here."

He said, "Look further down the canyon... way down behind us. See, that plume of smoke is from Blaine and Maggie's cabin. I left a good fire in the stove, so it'll be warm when they get there. You can't really see their cabin, itself, from here."

Annie nodded, as she gazed out over the land, caught in its stark, lonely beauty. This was her home now, and it would be easy to love. The wilderness and its solitude were soothing.

Kent broke into her thoughts, taking her chin into his hand and tilting it up. Dreamily, she saw his lips coming down to meet hers.

With no reservations, she met the demanding kiss, letting the rising heat from her loins flow through her lips. Her arms and lips clung, demanding fulfillment from him.

Kent tore his lips free. Shakily, he said, "Whew! I can't do anything about my problem here in the snow. Maybe we should head back down the ridge."

"Do you have a problem?" she inquired, slyly, sweetly, secretly delighted.

"You minx," he replied. "You know what the problem is."

And, indeed, she could see the huge bulge straining the front of his jeans, as he climbed back onto the snow machine.

Obediently, she climbed on the machine behind him and clasped her hands around his waist.

He groaned as she 'accidentally' brushed the bulge in the process.

Like a tumbleweed driven before storm winds, the snow machine tore down the ridge without stop, until the bridge in the birch grove was reached.

Kent stopped the machine a short ways before the bridge. He was coolly nonchalant – back in control. "Well here is the fishing hole," he said.

Annie subdued her sense of urgency. She did want to learn to fish, and, what is more, she wanted to let him play out his game of seduction... what she had slowly come to recognize as his tantalizing and teasing. Not cruelty at all... but a delicious sport.

She shivered. The cold was penetrating her clothing, for they had been out in it for quite some time.

Kent caught the motion. "Are you cold?" he asked, suddenly solictitous. At her nod, he said, "We can fix that." He went to a stack of split wood, brushed off the snow, and selected some smaller pieces.

Returning, he arranged them in a teepee above some pieces of papery birch bark. Flame from a lighter licked at the bark and grew.

Soon, Annie was warming her hands at a cheerful blaze and sipping a hot mug of coffee from a thermos he had brought.

He slipped up behind her, nibbling her ear and neck until she thought that she would lose her mind.

"Kent!" she protested, strong currents of lust curling in her. Somehow, she had to put an end to this torture.

"Ok, sweet heart," he said. He went to the stack of wood, twitched aside a tarpaulin against one side, and drew out a fly rod. A red and white, green winged artificial fly hook was already attached to the end of the line, a royal coachman, he told her over his shoulder.

He returned to her and took her hand, leading her onto the bridge. There, he put his arms around her from behind and, taking her hands in his, he positioned them on the rod and line.

Feeling his mastery of the act, she let him control her hands and arms, working the rod to flip out increasing amounts of line, until the fly settled to the surface of the water, at the head of a pool that lay up stream from the bridge.

The fly floated high on the water, moving with the current across the pool. His hands twitched the rod slightly, imparting a struggling, swimming motion to the artificial fly.

With a suddenness that caused her heart to leap, a large grayling darted from under the shelf of ice along the bank and snatched the fly, in an explosive splash of water.

Kent let go of her and said, "Now work him in to the bank and I will net him for you."

She began to pull in line, squealing excitedly each time the fish leapt out of the water, flopping and fighting, appearing to walk across the water on his tail, until she had worked the fish over to the bank above the bridge.

"Nice one," Kent complimented, as he scooped it up in the net.

She looked at the big grayling with a distinct sense of pride. She had caught her own dinner and it gave her a prideful feeling of self sufficiency.

When Kent suggested that she warm her hands by the fire, while he caught one more, she realized that her hands were numb from exposure to the cold water. She hadn't noticed them growing cold in the excitement of the contest.

The warmth of the flames was, at first, painful, then pleasurable, as she toasted her hands before the fire.

She watched him deftly capture the rest of their dinner. By the time he had scaled and gutted the fish, and rejoined her, the flames were dying low. It was time to go on to the cabin.

Kent carefully kicked the remnants of the fire into the creek to extinguish them. He leaned the fly rod back against the wood stack and covered it back up with its tarp.

A breathless sense of anticipation settled on her. It was time to go to the cabin... to become his wife, she was sure. Only the thinnest thread of doubt remained.

They walked to the snow machine. "Would you like to drive home?" he asked her.

Hesitantly, she replied, "Do you think I can... without wrecking us?"

He smiled. "Of course, you can," he replied, "Just go slow and easy. Follow the trail."

She climbed on the machine and sat down. He sat behind her – and she was pleasantly aware of his arms, tight around her waist. With a turn of the key, she started the machine.

Slowly, she drove off down the narrow trail. Why, this was not hard at all, as long as she kept going slow.

His lips found her neck. First there was the fluttering sensation of his warm breath, then delicate kisses and nibbles along both sides of her neck, a delicate nibbling at her ear lobes. In a heady turmoil, she squeezed the throttle tighter and the machine sped up.

She felt him slide his hands under her jacket. Gently he tugged her shirt tail free, and his hands were on her bare flesh.

He thrust his palm into her jeans and explored her bare flat belly, then let his hands creep up her rib cage to cup her breasts. Her nipples stiffened, almost painfully. He felt them, hard, pebble like against his palms.

Without conscious thought, she squeezed even tighter on the throttle.

They roared down the path, as tumultuous waves of sensation nearly overpowered her.

He began to brush his fingers back and forth against her nipples. The shocks of sensation echoed in her lips and groin.

She heard herself moan. The last thread of doubt parted, gently as a dewy spider web.

At last she saw the cabin, dimly, as though through a mist. She had thought she might not make it.

Annie stopped the machine in the yard and turned it off.

Kent dismounted, picked her up in his arms, and seemed to scorch her lips with his kiss. He trailed kisses down her neck.

"We were going pretty fast by the time we got here," he teased.

"Oh, take me inside," Annie moaned impatiently, and wriggled in his arms.

Kent carried her across the threshold and set her on her feet. With a kiss, he left her, turning his attention to lighting a fire in the stove.

Annie glanced at the thermometer. Twenty eight degrees, not too bad. She crossed the room and put a kettle of frozen water on the propane stove to be heated for hot chocolate.

Kent fed more wood into the flames and the room began to warm.

He turned, crossing the room to her, grasped her hand, and led her to stand with him beside the fire. Again he kissed her, as he stripped off her coat and hat.

He kicked off his boots and took off his own coat and hat, as Annie watched him.

Urgently, with unconscious power, she kicked off her own mukluks, and they flew across the room, thudding against the log walls.

There was no room for fear, as love and hot need surged in her blood stream. She felt bold and adventurous. *Now* was the time.

She sent him a beseeching glance, as she waited for him to continue.

Instead, he stretched and held his hands to the fire. He grinned, a lazy, sensuous grin. "What shall we do now?" he teased, "Shall we play a little scrabble? Or a game of cards?"

He really was cruel, she thought... a real sadist!

Tears of rage and urgency prickled in her eyes. "You are a *Beast*!" she cried. "Are you going to make me *show* you what game I want to play?"

Kent nodded, then watched, fascinated, as she began to unbutton her shirt. It hit the floor, in a heap, and her hands were at the waist of her long underwear shirt.

This had been worth waiting for.

She stripped the shirt off over her head and stood nude from the waist up.

Her breasts jutted defiantly, though her breasts and face and neck were crimson. Her bosom heaved, as she breathed heavily in passion.

"You are a blushing bride," he said with a laugh.

"Aren't you going to play the game?" she challenged. Her hands dropped to her belt buckle.

Kent was breathing hard as he crossed the room to her. He stripped her pants, long johns and socks from her in one motion.

Sweeping her up in his arms, he placed her gently on the eight foot bear-skin rug, before the stove. Soft fur embraced her back warmly. Sensuous, faintly tickling sensations from the silky black hairs heightened her anticipation, nearly unbearably.

She lay there, all fear or reluctance burned away in the fires of her womanhood. Through the veil of her half lowered eyelashes, she watched Kent unbutton his shirt, peel it off, and cast it to the floor.

His long muscular torso was gorgeous.

Her eyes opened wide, as he eased down the zipper of his jeans and the object causing the swelling in them burst forth.

Annie moaned as he pulled off his pants, and he joined her on the bear-skin. Tenderly, he began a detailed exploration of her body, finding little hidden places that leapt at his touch.

Something molten surged within her. Hotter and hotter.

Then she became an unthinking primitive, as the volcano pulsed, burst forth and engulfed them, consuming them totally in its fires.

When conscious thought returned, she lay spent, drained and conquered. Now she was a wife!

"Darling," she said. She kissed him, nestled into his strong arms, and dropped into an exhausted sleep.

Some time later, she woke, urgently ready, as awareness of his busy hands and mouth faded into her consciousness.

"What a marvelous way to wake up," she murmured to him, drowsily.

Fire crackled in the open stove, the flames casting flickering, surrealistic, orange light on their moving, sweat filmed bodies, turning and twisting on the silken fur. There was a dreamlike quality to what was happening to her, not quite yet fully awake.

He mounted her, and the rising rhythm of his gentle thrusts brought forth the ancient female rhythms buried in her instincts.

The sensations rose to a crescendo and burst, like the fountain of stars that climaxed the fourth of July fireworks display, and left her spent, clinging to him limply.

She felt filled with tenderness. "I love you, Darling, Mr. Winfield, my husband," she said and kissed his left ear, nibbling gently at the lobe.

Regretfully she placed another gentle kiss on his eye, now fading to black.

He stirred. "And I love you, Mrs. Winfield," he said. "It was even worth the black eye, to fetch you back. And, if you continue to measure up to tonights performance, I may even keep you."

Then he laughed at her irritated expression... "Dinner is nearly ready. I fixed it while you slept... to keep your energy up," he added meaningfully.

To his delight, a rosy blush started at the top of her bosom and rose in a red wave up her neck and face.

Dinner was a festive affair – and the fresh grayling, served on a warm plate... in their crisp fried crust of seasoned batter, were, as promised, a real treat. Crisp Chinese pea pods, in a light butter sauce, and golden home fried potatoes completed the satisfying repast.

Now, the future spread before them, a golden, glowing promise of joy in this Arctic land.

One last dark cloud remained... Juanita. One night, Kent began screaming and crying in his sleep, caught in the grip of his dream – for the last time. Annie, live, warm, wiggly, cuddly Annie, exorcised Juanita forever... and gained a better idea of what drove her man, in the process.

And so, a period of three weeks passed, an extraordinary part of it spent in bed.

At the end of that time the two couples journeyed to town, a merry journey this time. A shopping trip and night on the town were in prospect and, in a few short weeks, a trip to Hawaii.

A stop at the post office for their mail was a matter of course. They sat at one of the lodge's table enjoying coffee and pie, as they went through the mail.

"Kent," Blaine exclaimed, "You look like you're in a brown study. What's up?"

"Well, pardner, I've got this letter here from a publisher, back in Michigan... about my poems. Now, I was just speculating on how that could possibly come to be. I sure don't recollect sending any poems to a publisher."

"Oh, oh! Now look, I thought you owed it to yourself, to circulate your work. I had good intentions. I swear." Blaine was talking fast, nervously.

"What did they say?" Annie asked, "Is it good news or bad?" she seized the letter, scanned it rapidly, then squealed. "Oh, darling, they have sent a check for a thousand dollars grand prize in their contest and an offer of a contract for a book of your poems. I knew you could do it!" She threw her arms around him and kissed him thoroughly, oblivious to the grinning patrons at the other tables.

When she let him up for air, he said, "I've got to thank you, Blaine, for sending it in. I would never have found the courage to do it myself."

"Reckon I know how I'm going to spend some long winter hours this season," he added, with a laugh, "Trying for another contest win."

A little shyly, he pulled a paper from his coat pocket. I wrote another, in honor of the upcoming holidays. I had actually thought that I might enter it in the Fairbanks Daily News-Miner's Christmas poem competition.

With a happy grin, he read it:

A CHRISTMAS PLEA

Cookies, candy, things like that,
all contribute to my fat.
It doesn't seem quite fair to me,
that that's the way things should be.
Everything that's good to taste
ends up growing 'round my waist.
Furthermore, truth to tell,
I gain weight just from the smell.
Merry Christmas, the greeting sounds.
I just gained ten more pounds.
Santa, please, under the tree,
leave some will power just for me.

"I may never sell another one," he said, "but I'm having fun with them. We'll have to take that thousand dollars and do something extra special for Christmas, when we are in Hawaii."

"Hawaii!" shouted Annie, "Just being there will be extra special." A vision floated in her mind of white surf foaming over tropic sands, of golden sun in a blue sky silhouetting fringed palm trees.

It was a happy group that left the lodge to wend its way on toward town.

The two mail-order brides had a secret glow. But the cause of each other's glow was no secret to them.

With a woman's secret intuition, Annie and Maggie each saw in the other a new maturity, and the quiet serenity that comes to the woman who is pregnant with the child of a man whom she loves.

The husbands, of course, knew nothing. For isn't it true that the husband is always the last to know?

THE END

ABOUT THE AUTHOR

SugarPlum, Ted's wife, in front of the Leonard cabin 55 river miles up Alaska's Salcha River from the nearest road, the Richardson highway, which crosses the Salcha River 45 miles south of Fairbanks.

At right, Ted shows off his trapper's hat made of marten fur and his leather parka with wolf ruff. Avid hunters and fishermen, Ted and Plum spend most of their time at their Salcha River cabin.

Besides his novels and humor books, Ted writes the North Pole INDEPENDENT news-paper's outdoor page, regular columns for THE CURRENT DRIFT and free-lance for other papers. Ted is an award winning poet.

Coming soon: ALASKAN WILD LIFE, a collection of Alaskan humor, and ARE WE HAVING FUN YET? (for better or verse), Ted's collected Alaskan poetry.